"I charge five hundred a day, plus expenses, and I'd like a week in advance."
He wrote the check without blinking, tore it out, and handed it to me . . .

I took the check with as much nonchalance as I could muster. I had seen checks for more, but none that I had actually cashed . . .

"One more question," I said. "I thought you were staying with Connie, at the lake. Why can't you provide an alibi for her?"

"We sleep in separate bedrooms. And I'm afraid I sleep rather soundly. I couldn't swear that she didn't leave and come back in the night. Or, I suppose, any other time."

A definite disadvantage of drunken stupors. They destroy alibis. He made an attempt at a smile. All it did was twist his mouth.

"We must stay in touch, Miss O'Neal."

"Yeah, sure. Let me know when Connie gets out of jail."

He nodded and left.

I sat there at my desk and stared at the check. I had an awful feeling I was going to earn the money . . .

MORE MYSTERIES FROM THE
BERKLEY PUBLISHING GROUP . . .

INSPECTOR KENWORTHY MYSTERIES: Scotland Yard's consummate master of investigation lets no one get away with murder. "In the best tradition of British detective fiction!"—*Boston Globe*

by John Buxton Hilton

HANGMAN'S TIDE	CRADLE OF CRIME
FATAL CURTAIN	HOLIDAY FOR MURDER
PLAYGROUND OF DEATH	DEAD MAN'S PATH

DOG LOVER'S MYSTERIES STARRING JACKIE WALSH: She's starting a new life with her son and an ex-police dog named Jake . . . teaching film classes and solving crimes!

by Melissa Cleary
A TAIL OF TWO MURDERS

GARTH RYLAND MYSTERIES: Newsman Garth Ryland digs up the dirt in a serene small town—that isn't as peaceful as it looks . . . "A writer with real imagination!"—*The New York Times*

by John R. Riggs
HUNTING GROUND
HAUNT OF THE NIGHTINGALE
WOLF IN SHEEP'S CLOTHING

PETER BRICHTER MYSTERIES: A midwestern police detective stars in "a highly unusual, exceptionally erudite mystery series!"—*Minneapolis Star Tribune*

by Mary Monica Pulver

KNIGHT FALL	ORIGINAL SIN
THE UNFORGIVING MINUTES	
ASHES TO ASHES	

TEDDY LONDON MYSTERIES: A P.I. solves mysteries with a touch of the supernatural . . .

by Robert Morgan
THE THINGS THAT ARE NOT THERE

JACK HAGEE, P.I., MYSTERIES: Classic detective fiction with "raw vitality . . . Henderson is a born storyteller."—*Armchair Detective*

by C.J. Henderson
NO FREE LUNCH

FREDDIE O'NEAL, P.I., MYSTERIES: You can bet that this appealing Reno P.I. will get her man . . . "A winner."—Linda Grant

by Catherine Dain
LAY IT ON THE LINE
SING A SONG OF DEATH

SISTER FREVISSE MYSTERIES: Medieval mystery in the tradition of Ellis Peters . . .

by Margaret Frazer
THE NOVICE'S TALE

SING A SONG OF DEATH

▼

CATHERINE DAIN

JOVE BOOKS, NEW YORK

SING A SONG OF DEATH

A Jove Book / published by arrangement with
the author

PRINTING HISTORY
Jove edition / March 1993

ISBN: 0-515-11057-4

Jove Books are published by The Berkley Publishing Group,
200 Madison Avenue, New York, New York 10016.
The name "JOVE" and the "J" logo
are trademarks belonging to Jove Publications, Inc.

PRINTED IN THE UNITED STATES OF AMERICA

10 9 8 7 6 5 4 3 2 1

Chapter

1

"COME WITH ME, Freddie, it'll be fun, really it will," Sandra said.

"Watching an aging alcoholic make sexist jokes about chorus girls is not my idea of fun. He can't even sing anymore."

"Well, that part might not be fun, but the plane ride will be, and Lake Tahoe is beautiful in June, and you can do something else while I interview him."

"Planes are only fun if I get to fly them. I hate it when someone else has control."

I was starting to relent, though. I did like the idea of flying up to Lake Tahoe—which is beautiful all the time, creeping pollution be damned—seeing the floor show at the Sultan's Seraglio hotel-casino, spending the night, and flying back. Not to mention maybe three meals. All on the *Nevada Herald*—or the Seraglio, I wasn't quite sure which—because Sandra Herrick was going to interview the headliner. And I'd never flown a Learjet. Maybe if the pilot was a nice guy, he'd let me take the controls. Taking a Learjet from Reno to Lake Tahoe was some kind of overkill, of course, but evidently the Sultan, or somebody, was out to impress Vince Marina, who was flying back to Reno in it, with us, the following day.

"So what'll you do tomorrow if you don't go?"

"I thought I might straighten out my office. I'm a little behind on my filing."

"Oh, good. You've decided to go."

"What time are we leaving?"

"I'll pick you up at ten. We don't meet with Vince Marina until four, so we can just enjoy the lake for a few hours."

"*You* meet with Vince Marina at four. I'll enjoy the lake for a few more hours."

"All right, whatever. I'll see you tomorrow at ten."

I hung up the phone and wished I had asked her a few more questions. Such as why, really, Sandra was interviewing Vince Marina. Sandra Herrick was a political reporter first and foremost, with a secondary interest in crime. Life-style was not her beat. Vince Marina had sung once at the White House—he had switched from the Democratic party to the Republican sometime around 1980, when an actor in the Oval Office made it the thing to do—and there were the usual rumors of Mafia ties that accompany any entertainer from New Jersey who makes it big, but I couldn't think of anything that would make him a story, make him news, make him someone Sandra would want to interview. And I couldn't think why she would want me to go with her. Okay, we're friends, but not that close. Even figuring she knew I was between cases, which meant I had some free time and could use a free meal.

And to tell the truth, much as I like Sandra, when the phone had rung at three o'clock on a Monday afternoon, I was hoping for a client.

I looked at my desk. Actually, the line about being behind on my filing was true. I run a one-woman private investigation service out of what used to be the living room of my house, doing mostly skip tracing and other small jobs, and the best word to describe both my housekeeping and my clerical skills is inept. I keep as much of the office work on my computer as I can, but there still seem to be papers that land on my desk for one reason or another, and I can't figure out what to do with them, so they stay there.

I stacked the papers arbitrarily into neat piles. At least the desk looked better. I found a buried city directory and returned it to the bookcase, but I couldn't figure out where to start straightening books, so I stuck it into a shelf edgewise. My framed Union Pacific poster was askew. That was easy to straighten and gave me a feeling of accomplishment.

Butch jumped onto my desk, flicking his gray plume of a tail, and that was the end of two stacks.

The hell with it. If the papers were a mess again, it must be the will of Allah. I ran through the game directory on my hard disk, settled on Star Trek, and battled Klingons and Romulans until my legs had gone to sleep with the weight of two cats—Sundance had joined the party, and Butch had generously let him stay—and I was thinking about food.

I fed the cats before I left. Reno is still close enough to open country that it's an easy town to forage in, and I hate to come home to leftover bits of rats, birds, or—worst of all—bats. Nobody eats the wings.

The sun was setting as I walked down Mill toward Virginia Street, dangling a denim jacket I would need for the walk back. The day had been clear, and the sky was all pinks and purples, with none of the bright smog red that shows up more and more often as the city grows. Early June is a great time in Reno. Late May is probably a little better—the tourist season officially starts on Memorial Day weekend—but in early June everything is still green, the days are mild, and the nights rarely drop below forty. A few lilacs are still hanging on, and the roses are in full bloom.

Mill Street was quiet, residential, and badly in need of regentrification. It was too close to downtown to attract anyone but transients, and the frame houses all showed the effects of too many harsh winters. My house was a half block off Mill, conveniently close to the police station, and it, too, was in need of more attention than I was giving it. I thought about a new coat of paint, but it just wasn't in my budget.

I turned right on Virginia, and within a block I had lost the sunset to a harsh neon haze. The Barrington Hotel was still a dark spot on the otherwise glittery street. I wondered if it would ever reopen. Once past it, I slipped into the eddy of flashing lights, ringing buzzers, and spilling coins that was the tourists' Reno. I couldn't really knock it—tourism was the biggest industry in the state, the source of one out of every three jobs, and without it, we might have had something worse. I would have to think about what that might have been.

The Mother Lode was one of the older casinos, small enough to feel comfortable and homelike. I crossed the forced air barrier—no need for doors when you're open twenty-four hours a day—and worked my way through the maze of tables to the escalator. The owners understood their customers. No straight aisles, and the food was on the second floor. Temptations to the right, lures to the left, inexpensive food upstairs. That, of course, was the saving grace of it all for me. I could eat fairly well fairly inexpensively, thanks to the tourists who subsidized the food by pausing for one not-so-brief moment at the slot machines.

I took my seat at the counter, nodded to Diane, the waitress, and reached for a Keno ticket.

"Hamburger and a beer?" Diane asked, moving to my end after serving what appeared to be breakfast to an unshaven elderly guy with the shakes about halfway down.

"Yeah, sure." I randomly marked eight numbers and pulled out a dollar.

Diane nodded and left to turn in my order. She was plumpish, fortyish, and reasonably attractive, in a motherly way, and I had never asked her how she ended up as a counter waitress at the Mother Lode, even though I had eaten there two or three times a week for as long as I could remember.

A perky young Keno runner, someone I hadn't seen before, smiled cheerfully as she picked up my ticket and my dollar.

"Good luck," she said.

I nodded in surprise. The tired, aching woman she replaced had never noticed my existence.

I drank half a beer waiting for my hamburger and watching for my game to come up. I thought about Vince Marina. In the early sixties, he was the voice of cool jazz. If

Miles was the trumpet, Coltrane the sax, Vince was the voice. Not that I remembered those days. My father was a big jazz fan, and when he split, he left his records behind. There was a time when I played them a lot.

Vince Marina had gone platinum with a couple of records, a collection of Christmas carols and one of Broadway hits. When a lot of the jazz joints closed in the seventies, he did some concert tours, then gravitated to the saloon circuit with a mainstream act. For the last few years he hadn't done much except for two weeks in Reno, two in Vegas, and two at Tahoe. But he probably got fifty grand a week, and I imagined he could live on that. I still didn't understand why Sandra wanted to interview him.

"You never gonna win at that game. You oughta just quit."

I jumped but didn't turn, because I had just hit three numbers and was hoping for more. I didn't get them.

"Goddamn it, Deke," I said when the board had stopped lighting up, "that was bad luck. You should have said, 'Baby needs shoes!' That wins every time."

"Bullshit. Keno is a sucker game."

Deke settled onto the stool next to me. He looked at me through small, red-rimmed eyes in a black, pear-shaped face that topped a black, pear-shaped body. A large pear, like the pear that ate Chicago. Deke—Deacon Adams—was a former air-force survival instructor, now a security guard at the Mother Lode, and probably my closest friend, although it would have embarrassed him if I said so.

Diane took his order for a steak, salad, fries, and a beer.

"Do you know anything about Vince Marina?" I asked.

"Just I heard he might be looking for a bodyguard."

"Why?"

Deke shrugged. "Why would anybody be looking for a bodyguard? I didn't ask, because I didn't want the job. Probably you don't want it either."

"You're probably right. And I haven't been offered the job anyway."

"Then why're you asking about Vince Marina?"

"Because I'm flying up to Lake Tahoe with Sandra Herrick tomorrow. She's interviewing Vince, and I was wondering why."

"Probably you should have asked her that."

I glared at him.

"Probably I will."

"Same card again?" the Keno runner asked sweetly.

"Yeah, sure."

I gave her another dollar.

"I don't want the next time I hear from you to be a phone call asking will I feed your cats while you're up there at Lake Tahoe being Vince Marina's bodyguard, you hear me?"

"I hear you. Don't worry about it. That's not what I'm going up there for. I'm just going because Don is tied up at work and Sandra wanted company and she asked me."

Deke looked at me steadily.

"Why you?"

"I guess you'll have to ask her."

I finished my dinner and left. I was feeling a little annoyed with Sandra. If she hoped Vince Marina would hire me as his bodyguard so that she could get some kind of inside story on why he needed one, she could have told me up front. Not that it mattered. People like Vince Marina didn't hire female private investigators as bodyguards. They hired big guys with puffy ears whose noses were so flat they had to breathe through their mouths, guys who broke kneecaps on Sunday afternoons for the sport of it. I might be able to break a kneecap if I had to—I wear cowboy boots with reinforced toes, and kneecaps give easily if you approach them from the side—but the thought made me a little queasy. Bodyguarding was out.

I detoured a couple of blocks out of my way to the neighborhood video store. There wasn't much I hadn't seen, except for the teen comedies that I've never been able to watch more than five minutes of, so I ended up in the Classics section and picked up *Julius Caesar,* the old Marlon Brando version. Politics and crime. Almost as certain as death and taxes.

"Is this any good?" the redheaded kid at the checkout counter asked.

"It's great," I told him. "You could watch it once a year for the rest of your life."

"Yeah? I'll have to try it."

Butch and Sundance were waiting for me on the porch. They dashed ahead of me into the kitchen when I opened the door, but I didn't plan on giving them anything more, just getting a beer for myself. They followed reluctantly into the bedroom. I drank a beer, watched the movie, drank another beer and watched another movie on cable, and fell asleep late enough that the alarm jerked all three of us awake at eight in the morning.

I threw a swimming suit, a good blouse, a long T-shirt to sleep in, and a change of underwear into a canvas bag and was waiting when Sandra arrived. I tossed the bag into the backseat of her Toyota Cressida.

"I want to know the whole story," I said. "I want to know why you're interested in Vince Marina."

She looked at me in mock innocence. She was wearing an ivory jumpsuit with a flowered scarf and her usual heavy gold jewelry. What the *Vogue* model wears on a Learjet. Her blond hair was carefully styled, more in the manner of the TV anchor she could have been than the newspaper reporter she was. As usual, I felt like the country mouse in my western-style blue shirt and Levi's. But even in Levi's— and I've never seen her in Levi's—Sandra would be gorgeous, and I don't compete with gorgeous.

"I told you. I'm interviewing him."

"Right. But why? And don't say somebody has to. Deke told me last night that Vince is looking for a bodyguard."

Sandra got very busy driving until she turned south onto the freeway, toward the airport. I waited.

"Vince isn't exactly looking for a bodyguard. His friend and manager, Benny Elcano, is trying to convince him to hire one. His ex-wife is threatening to kill him."

"That's a week's worth of 'Oprah'—ex-wives who threaten to kill their ex-husbands."

"The rumor is that this particular one has already tried a

couple of times and failed, and that for some reason Vince won't go to the police, won't get an injunction against her.''

''How do you know?''

''Because Benny Elcano's sister, Juanita Elcano Holt, is Governor Reilly's personal assistant. You might remember her mother—she used to teach eighth grade at Central.''

I nodded. I wasn't in Mrs. Elcano's homeroom, but I remembered her.

''And Juanita thought I might look into it, as a personal favor, off the record. I didn't tell her it was out of my league.''

''You called me instead. As a personal favor.''

''Something like that.''

''That's fine, Sandra, and I'll do whatever I can. I just think you should have told me the whole story.''

''Well, I was going to.''

''When?''

''When I had to. I was hoping you'd get up there and meet him and he'd hire you, and it would all happen naturally.''

''Sure. He's gonna love me.''

Sandra drove and I sulked the short distance to the charter terminal just south of Cannon International. I grabbed my bag, got out, and continued to sulk while she retrieved her garment sack and makeup case from the trunk. We walked to the office, and I didn't offer to help her carry anything. The Sultan's Seraglio pilot was waiting. I nodded to Jerry McIntire, who was waiting with him. Jerry nodded back. He checked me out whenever I flew, which was as often as I could find an excuse. I used to see a lot of his brother, and things had been a little tense between us when Rob married somebody else, but we were pretty much over that.

Jerry made the introductions. The pilot, Dean Sawyer, was in his forties, graying and macho, probably a 'Nam vet. I didn't bother to ask if I could sit in the cockpit with him.

When I saw the silver beauty we were flying in, I almost stopped sulking. *Odalisque* was calligraphed on her side. Sandra and I climbed into the cabin—more like a lounge— settled into two of the luxurious leather seats, the color of fresh blood and the texture of soft butter, fastened our belts, and I decided to relax and enjoy.

"Okay," I said, "you win. This is fun. But why do we rate the Learjet?"

"I told you. Vince is flying to Reno tomorrow, for a United Way lunch. He's honorary chair of this year's fund-raising. We get the ride up because the plane was here for servicing."

"Jesus. Corporate America spends a small fortune flying Vince Marina from Lake Tahoe to Reno—a fortune they could have given to the United Way, if they didn't have anything better to do with it—and we're along for the ride. No wonder we're losing to the Japanese."

"Freddie, that's enough. Look out the window or something."

I barely had time. And the view wasn't much more than a blur. Taking off, circling toward the mountains, and landing at the lake took maybe fifteen minutes. A stunning fifteen minutes, the water sparkling like a star sapphire almost the whole time as we zoomed over it and down to the small airport in Tahoe Valley, on the California side of the lake, about six miles from Stateline, a collection of monstrous gambling dens that likes to be called Lake Tahoe. As if the rest of the lake doesn't count.

A stretch limo painted an ostentatious gold and a driver—a short, balding man dressed in black, who didn't volunteer any words—were waiting to ferry us to the Seraglio.

We took the narrow road through the tall pines, and I watched for the first icy white shaft of light, followed by a blast of clear blue, that meant we were nearing the lake. But all I caught was a first glimpse of purity. Then we were into the tacky land of hamburger stands, motels, and wedding chapels. Just across the state line the landscape erupted into high rise.

The Nevada side of Lake Tahoe, The City, had to be one of the ugliest spots on earth. Huge, garish buildings jammed next to each other, neon flashing day and night. When Joni Mitchell sang "pave paradise, put up a parking lot," she might have been thinking of Lake Tahoe. The Seraglio was the worst of the lot, the biggest and the gaudiest. If there had been an Anti–Turkish Defamation League, they would have sued over the neon-turbaned muscleman waving a neon scimitar over the doorway. Our limo rolled up into the line of two other limos—trust me, three stretch limos make a line—at the entrance to the lobby.

Sandra announced our presence to the registration clerk, who gave her a card to sign and gave our room key to the young man who had grabbed her garment bag as the driver took it out of the limo's trunk. He ushered me through a red-and-gold lobby surprisingly devoid of slot machines and up to a suite on the tenth floor. By this time I was tense and uncomfortable again. I tried to remember the last time I had stayed in a hotel. Probably four years earlier, when I had my house fumigated, but that was a Motel 6. And I had never seen a hotel room like this one except in movies.

The wall across from the door was glass, with a sliding door leading onto a small, concrete balcony that held a couple of chaises. I walked over and looked out at lake and trees and mountains and sky, all blue and green and purple and white, and as overwhelming as a sudden orchestral burst in a symphony. When you see high clouds that start at snow-covered mountaintops and sweep up from there, you get a whole new perspective on space.

I turned back to a room that was only disappointing by comparison. There was a muted ivory-and-rose brocade couch and a couple of matching chairs, an entertainment center, and a wet bar. A large basket of fruit wrapped in gold cellophane sat on a low table in front of the couch.

"Wow," I said, when Sandra had graciously dispatched the young man. "How do people live like this?"

"Very well. They live very well. You want lunch by the pool?"

"Oh, hey, why not?"

The other room of our suite held two queen-size beds with brocade spreads, a large dresser, a closet with a mirrored door, and another opening to the balcony.

We changed into our swimsuits. Sandra wrapped hers

with a sarong that might have graced Esther Williams, and I put my blue shirt back on over mine. We took the elevator down to the glass-enclosed pool, which was actually on the fifth floor, on top of the casino. One side of it was roped off for tables and umbrellas. A friendly waiter took our order, and I began to think of this as a vacation.

The vacation feeling continued after lunch. We swam, lay in the heated sunlight—on the other side of the glass the sun was bright, but the air was no warmer than sixty-five—then got dressed and took the hotel shuttle down to the beach to walk in the sand. I walked close enough to the water that I could reach down and let the waves lap my fingers, but to go in Lake Tahoe in early June, you have to be part polar bear, and I am not. I never liked the temperature of the water even in August—and I had been to Lake Tahoe a lot in August. I used to come every summer to the YWCA camp at Zephyr Cove, just a couple of miles north of Stateline.

I have some vague memories of weaving plastic key chains, singing a song about being happy while I was hiking, and toasting marshmallows over a campfire, but I don't remember ever liking it very much.

The limo and driver were sitting in front of the hotel at quarter to four, ready to drive us to the private house owned by the Seraglio for the use of their stars. I went along because I couldn't figure out anything else to do. I didn't want to wander on the beach any longer, and I don't gamble except for a couple of Keno tickets with dinner, and there just didn't seem to be much else available. I thought about taking a ride on a Mississippi-style steamer that looked like a set for *Show Boat,* but I would have felt dumb and touristy.

We drove almost to the Y camp, turned into a private drive that ran along the beach, and parked in front of an improbable two-story Swiss alpine house. The door flew open.

"Hey, I'm glad to see you girls, come on in," said a small olive-skinned man wearing a maroon sport shirt buttoned to his neck and black slacks. He nervously brushed one hand over the thinning dark hair on his head. The furrows in his forehead gave him a permanent expression of puzzled anxiety. "I'm Benny Elcano."

I looked for a resemblance to his mother. I guess there was a little of it in the puzzled anxiety.

Sandra introduced us, and he shook first her hand and then mine. We followed him into a larger version of the living room of our suite, including a formal dining area at one end. Vince Marina was standing by the door to the balcony, cigarette in one hand, glass in the other. The liquid was clear, and could have been ice water. I just doubted it.

I had to admit he was still a handsome man. He was tall, over six feet, and his blue polo shirt covered muscles just losing their definition and a belly just going soft. His thick salt-and-pepper hair reflected the late-afternoon sun. It wasn't until he stepped back from the window that I could see the dissipation in his tanned face, heavy Mediterranean features sagging at eye and chin.

"How do you do, Mr. Marina. I'm Freddie O'Neal."

I strode forward, holding out my hand. I was not going to be intimidated.

"Call me Vince, honey. Are you the reporter?"

He moved his glass to the hand that held the cigarette, knocking ashes to the carpet, grasped my hand briefly, and dropped it. His eyes were big and brown and swimming in something, and I was certain the glass wasn't ice water.

"No, sir. Vince. I'm just along for the ride."

Sandra was next to me by that time, and she took over. Benny bustled off to see about drinks—a beer for me, an iced tea for Sandra, and more of whatever Vince was drinking.

Sandra and Vince sat on the couch, she gushed a little while she pulled out a tape recorder and turned it on, and they started to talk. I followed Benny.

A short hall led to a kitchen the size of my whole house. Wolfgang Puck would shit his pants if he saw it. An oven you could roast a side of beef in. A butcher-block table for half a dozen butchers to work side by side. Benny was leaning against said butcher block, watching an Oriental guy dressed in white arranging glasses on a tray.

"Hi—Freddie, wasn't it?"

"Yeah."

I continued to gawk at the kitchen.

"You said you're not a reporter. So what do you do?"

"I'm a private investigator."

"Really? A girl like you? I mean, you're a big girl, and you look like you can take care of yourself, but . . ."

He trailed off and I didn't help him out. He hit "big" just a little too hard. I'm tall and what might be called rawboned, and I can take care of myself, but "big" sounds overweight, which I am not. I've never liked being called "big."

When I decided he had looked at the floor long enough, I said, "I heard Vince might be looking for a bodyguard. A private one, who wouldn't attract a lot of attention."

"Well, yeah, I made a few inquiries, but—"

This time I cut him off.

"I'm not looking for a job. But I have a friend who might be."

Private investigators learn to lie at an early age.

"Look, Vince just has a few problems with his ex-wife, no big deal."

I stared. He continued.

"Except for the time she threw a knife at him. And her trying to run him down with the truck, twice I think it was. But he won't do nothing about it. I begged him to get an injunction, but he won't do it."

"Why?"

"Hey, if he told me, I would tell you. He just don't take it too seriously."

His mother would have made him stay after school for talking that way. Bad grammar was her pet peeve.

"If he doesn't, why do you?"

"Because I was there when she was chasing him down the street in the truck, and that woman means it. She ain't gonna quit until he's dead."

He picked up the tray, and I followed him back to the living room.

Benny and I both sat there with glazed eyes while Sandra chatted with Vince for an hour or so about nothing that interested either one of them. Then Benny said something about Vince having to rest before the show, and we all made polite good-byes, ending with Vince insisting we come backstage after the show.

Sandra waited until we got back in the room before she asked me what Benny said.

"Not much," I told her. "Just what you already know—his ex-wife is trying to kill him. And he isn't taking it seriously. Until he does, there's nothing anyone else can do."

Changing for the show didn't take me much time. I put on the white silk blouse that was the dressiest thing I owned, brushed out my hair, and replaced the rubber band that held it at the nape of my neck. Sandra took longer to put on a flowered, full-skirted summer dress and jacket and redo makeup that looked fine to me the way it was. She scrutinized me carefully.

"A silk blouse with jeans is always good. You can wear it almost anywhere. A simple gold chain. That's all you need to go with it, just a simple gold chain."

She whipped one out of her makeup case and fastened it around my neck. I looked in the mirror. My nose was peeling. But I kind of liked the chain.

"Thanks. It helps."

The evening was better than I expected. The prime rib was rare and the show was okay. The opening was one of those flashy chorus numbers—this one had an Old West theme, cowboys hunting female Indians in bikinis, and a spectacular finish with a lot of dancers dying. And Vince Marina had been doing his act so long he could have done it in his sleep. He almost did. But I was wrong about one thing. He could still sing. He sat on a bar stool with a mike in his hand and a single spot on him for forty-five minutes, and nobody in the audience made a sound—except for a few chuckles at the old jokes—until the end. Drinks sat untouched, cigarettes unsmoked. And actually, there was only one sexist chorus-girl joke. The guy really was good.

Benny came to escort us backstage afterward. Vince's dressing room was so crowded with people that I just took a beer from the bar—there was a full bar at one end—and retreated to a corner while Sandra worked the room. Everybody looked about fifty. The men were graying and overweight, wearing open-necked shirts and expensive sport jackets. The women had dyed hair and heavy makeup and wore even more gold jewelry than Sandra. I wondered what they all did.

"Cherry bombs are the latest craze," one of the women was saying. "You simply can't leave your shoes by the pool anymore, or the next thing you know, someone has blown them up."

I couldn't figure it out. Was that supposed to be fun?

I put my beer down and left. I wandered out to the lounge, played a couple of Keno tickets while a black rhythm-and-blues group did their act, and finally got bored enough that I decided I might be tired.

Sandra was already in the room, in her nightgown.

"You could have said something to him, at least how much you liked his show."

"Everybody tells him that. He didn't need me to."

"Tomorrow on the plane. You'll have another chance tomorrow on the plane."

"Sandra, he doesn't want to hire anybody, and I don't want the job."

She said a short good night and pulled the covers up around her head.

Sandra seemed to fall asleep almost immediately. I missed my cats. I moved to the other room and turned on the television set. I finally drifted to sleep on the couch.

Vince and Benny were already in the limo when it stopped for us the next morning. I hate mornings, and Vince apparently had a hangover, because he had dark glasses on and stared out the window, ignoring us, so Sandra chatted with Benny about Vince's schedule the short distance to the airport. They agreed that she should join them at the United Way lunch. I did my best to crawl into the cushions so no one would ask me. No one did.

Dean Sawyer was waiting at the plane for us, all checked

out, smugly drinking coffee from a thermos cup. I hoped there was more coffee on the plane. The one cup I'd had at the hotel hadn't been enough. He nodded at us as we climbed into the cabin.

I was impressed again, belting myself into the big, soft seat. Sandra and Vince had taken the windows, Benny and I the aisles, which didn't make the conversation smoother, since Vince and I were still doing our own versions of not being there.

There was not only coffee, there was a flight attendant to serve it. She was young and blond and bubbly and cute, wearing a gold miniskirt and jacket with a red blouse and tights. The pilot had just let us know over the intercom that she could move about the cabin, but he would rather the rest of us stayed in our seats for the short trip, when she let us know how thrilled she was to be pouring coffee for Vince Marina. She was less thrilled to be pouring for the rest of us, but she did it anyway.

I could have learned to love that plane. I wondered if Sawyer took it joyriding around the west when his corporate bosses had no other plans for it. I would have given odds that he did. Turned on the autopilot and impressed the girls.

I didn't have a chance to ask him. We had barely leveled out at the north end of the lake when the door to the cockpit opened and Sawyer stumbled out, white-faced. He moved his mouth, trying to say something, and then pitched forward onto the carpet.

I was out of my seat and over to him, checking his neck for a pulse, before anyone else moved.

"Is he all right?" Sandra gasped.

"Oh, my God!" the attendant wailed.

"His pulse is good, but his skin is cold, and I think he may be out for a while."

"How do we get out of this?" Benny whispered, almost as white as Sawyer.

"Oh, don't worry about that," Sandra said brightly. "Freddie's a pilot—she can land the plane. Can't you?"

"Somebody cover him with a blanket, keep him warm, he may snap back."

I didn't want to answer her. I got up and walked into the cockpit, sat down in the pilot's seat. Sandra followed.

"Sit down and close the door," I ordered.

She sat in the copilot's seat.

"You can land the plane, can't you?" she asked again, with a little less confidence in her voice. "You do have a pilot's license."

"I also have a driver's license. But that doesn't mean if somebody dropped me into an Indy car going two hundred miles an hour and told me to take it into the pit safely, I could do it. Sandra, this is a jet. I've never flown a jet. I fly Cherokees, little planes, at about a third of this speed. If I try to take it down, I could kill us all."

She looked at me firmly.

"I'm certain you can do it. What do I do to help?"

I flipped the approach book open to Reno/Cannon and handed it to her.

"Look in here for the Reno tower frequency and dial it in." I dialed it in all the time. All of a sudden I couldn't remember what it was. But it gave Sandra something to do while I looked at the unfamiliar instrument panel.

Some things looked familiar. At least I could tell I was in a plane. Sawyer had known he was passing out in time to turn the IFF Squawk to 7700, the emergency frequency, as well as turn on the autopilot. The Reno tower would be expecting to hear from us. I touched the unfamiliar yoke. I was going to have to turn the autopilot off soon.

"I've got it," Sandra said.

I picked up the mike.

"Reno tower, this is the *Odalisque* declaring an in-flight emergency, the pilot is unconscious."

"This is Reno tower. Who are you, *Odalisque*?"

"I don't know the call letters. The jet is owned by the Sultan's Seraglio. My name is Freddie O'Neal. Does anybody there know how to land a Learjet?"

There was a silence at the other end. Then a burst of static, and the voice was back.

"This is Reno tower. We've called the National Guard, and we'll patch you through to the supervisor."

There was another burst of static, and a new male voice.

"This is Conrad. What's going on?"

"This is O'Neal. I'm in a Learjet about twelve thousand feet up, passing over Mount Rose. The pilot is out. How do I land?"

"Are you instrument qualified, O'Neal?"

"Yes, sir." I had decided I had to be instrument qualified about a year after I got my license, when I had been trapped once too often at the Reno airport because the inversion layer had fogged in the airport, even though the mountains were clear. Instrument qualified meant I could take off and land using the ILS, the Instrument Landing System.

"Then we'll give it a shot. How's your fuel?"

"No problem with the fuel."

"Take the jet out east of Reno and fly until you start feeling comfortable with the way it handles. Slow it to one twenty knots, set the power to seventy-eight percent, and trim it up so it'll fly. Stabilize at that power and airspeed. We'll try to keep everyone out of your way."

"Take it out on vector 060," the tower voice broke in.

Sweat was running down my armpits. I switched off the autopilot, took the yoke, and started to turn right to 060.

"How do I trim?" I yelled.

"The plane has an electronic trim, O'Neal. Upper right corner of the yoke, you can hit it with your right thumb."

I did as told. It was as if power steering had just clicked in.

"You see?" Sandra said. "This is going to be just fine."

I could feel the power of the jet under my hands. I was too scared to answer her. I hit 060 and headed east toward the desert. I might have to go all the way to New York to feel comfortable.

"How we doing, girls?" Benny stuck his head around the cockpit door. "Everything all right in here?"

"No problem, Benny," Sandra said. "We're just taking the long way home."

"We thought we might break out the drinks, if we're going to be up here for a while. Sawyer doesn't seem to be coming around. Can I bring anybody anything?"

"No, thank you, we'll let you know if we need anything."

Sandra was smiling, I could hear it in her voice, even though I couldn't turn to look at her. I was biting my lower lip to keep from yelling at them.

He backed out and shut the door.

By the time I spotted Fernley, I was as comfortable as I was going to get. Which wasn't very. It was how I imagined riding a dragon—I wasn't sure which of us was in control— but at least I could have counted on the dragon not hurting himself when he landed.

"Conrad, are you there?"

"I'm here, O'Neal."

"What do we do next?"

"Reno tower, this is Conrad, patch in Approach Control."

"You have it—and they're briefed."

"Make a left turn, O'Neal, descend to 10,500 feet, and dial the ILS, that's 109.6."

"This is Approach Control, fly heading 300 to intercept the ILS to Runway 16. The altimeter is 30.10."

Fernley was gone. We were briefly back over the desert, and I saw the red tiles of the Spanish Springs housing development. This was all happening too damn fast.

"This is Approach Control, descend to eighty-five hundred feet and turn left to 180."

"This is Conrad, O'Neal, dial the ILS course to 164. Hold at eighty-five hundred and watch for the needle to come off the case. Use the glide slope to control your descent to the runway."

"What's he talking about?" Sandra whispered.

"There—that window. The needle that comes from the side is the course, and the one that comes from the bottom is the glide slope. We want them to center. That'll mean we've found the ILS beam."

"Isn't this exciting?"

I couldn't find the words to answer her.

"This is O'Neal. The glide slope needle is rising."

"This is Conrad. Trim it up, drop the flaps, start your

descent. Maintain your speed at 120 knots. Follow the glide slope and keep aiming for the runway."

"How fast are we going?" Sandra asked.

"Try two miles per minute."

"Don't we slow down to land?"

"Not much."

"O'Neal, this is Conrad, have you dropped your landing gear?"

"What?"

"Your landing gear."

"Oh, God. Thanks."

I looked for the lever to drop the landing gear, and a new rush of fear swept me. The Cherokee had fixed gear, I never had to drop it. What else would be different? What else wouldn't I think of?

I concentrated on the small instrument window, keeping the needles centered.

"O'Neal, you're wandering around the glide slope. Don't chase the needle. Small changes will do it."

"Yes, sir. Thank you."

My hands were slippery, and I thought they might be shaking. I consciously relaxed my grip on the yoke.

"All right, O'Neal, you're about five miles out, on course. Look for the runway and pick your spot to land."

"Sandra, once we're on the ground, I need you to look for the distance markers on the runway. When you see one, call out the number to me."

We were hurtling toward the earth.

And then we were over the threshold.

"Pull back, pull back!" Conrad shouted. "Look at the end of the runway and pull back!"

I pulled back on the yoke with what I hoped was a smooth, even pull. The wheels thunked onto the runway. I stomped on the brakes and almost lost control when the nose gear slapped onto the concrete.

"I see a marker," Sandra cried. "Nine thousand." She followed that almost too quickly with "seven thousand."

I focused on the end of the runway and leaned on the brakes. Fifty knots at the end of the runway will kill you.

"Five thousand. Three thousand."

I watched the needle fall below fifty. We were going to stop.

"Good going, O'Neal," the radio barked, and echoed twice more.

"Marvelous," Sandra bubbled. "You were just marvelous. I knew you could do it."

I sat there and slumped over the yoke. My deodorant had failed, and I was conscious of the stink of my body. I saw a truck out of the corner of my eye, and I knew people were running up to the plane.

The door to the cockpit opened.

"Vince said to tell you thanks for landing the plane, honey," Benny said. "Great job. Don't worry, he'll be in touch."

Chapter

2

I DISCOVERED IN childhood what lousy human beings famous people can be. When I was ten, my father took me to the rodeo, just the two of us, and he even bought box seats so we could really see what was going on. Not that the Washoe County Fairgrounds, where the rodeo was held, was that big anyway. But the day started out to be special, sitting in a box with my father, listening to him make small bets with the people around us and joke about the Reno mayor, who came in at a gallop, waving his hat in one hand, with the other firmly clutching the saddle horn. I could smell the dust and the sweat and the horses, pick up the tension in the crowd when a rider was thrown from a Brahma and the clowns had to distract everyone until the rider was carried out on a stretcher.

Rodeos are even closer to the old Roman gladiator games than football. Maybe not closer than boxing—about the same. The idea is, people get hurt for other people's amusement. At ten, with my father making jokes, I couldn't feel the pain, and I saw it as a strange, fascinating celebration of the Old West. It's still alive, a small but persistent subculture that has never acknowledged the twentieth century and probably won't acknowledge the twenty-first either. But I don't really know much about it—I haven't gone to a rodeo since that one. I don't even like the movie where Robert Mitchum gets a stomped lung.

Sitting in the next box were some television people, stars

of a TV western series. They had a crew filming some footage for the following season—that's how little rodeos have changed in a hundred years—but mostly they were just hanging out. One of the actresses, a regular on the series who has since become a star, began flirting with my father. She was asking him all about Reno and the rodeo, laughing at his jokes, taking his small bets and losing. She ignored me. By the end of the afternoon, so did he. He drove me home, kissed me on the cheek, and told me to tell Mom he'd be home a little later. A little later was three days, when the TV people went back to Los Angeles.

I always thought the fight they had when he came home was the beginning of the end. The end, of course, was the time he didn't come back.

So I didn't really expect to hear from Vince Marina. And I almost fell off my chair when the phone rang the next day and I answered it and Benny said, "Vince wants to offer you a job, just for the time he's here at the lake. How soon can you get up here?"

"A job doing what?"

"Looking out for him a little. Seeing that nothing like the airplane thing happens again."

"I don't even know how 'the airplane thing' happened the first time."

"Yeah, well, maybe you could check into that, too."

I thought for a minute. I really did want an excuse to ask some questions, since I almost got killed.

"Four hundred a day," I said.

"No problem."

"Plus expenses."

"Yeah, sure. When can you get here?"

I should have asked for five.

"In time for dinner. I just have a couple of things to take care of first."

"Fine. We'll see you then."

I hung up the phone and picked it up again. My first phone call was to Washoe Medical Center, looking for Dean Sawyer, but he had already been released. So I called the charter terminal, hoping Jerry McIntire could give me a lead on him. Jerry had an address and phone number in Sparks.

"I hear you did some pretty fancy flying yesterday," he said. "Dean'll probably want to thank you for saving his plane."

I decided not to call Sawyer, but to drive out there and take a chance. I made one more phone call.

"Hey, Deke, how'd you like to feed my cats for a few days?"

The address Jerry gave me was a town house in one of those jumbled complexes where you have to wander around looking for the right letter on the door and "F" never seems to follow "E" in the direction you expect it to. There was a lot of dark wood casting shadows, and it wasn't the kind of place where I'd want to come home alone at night.

The woman who answered the door was in her late thirties, smooth looking in a light cotton shirt and jeans. She looked as if she normally went to work in a suit, but this just wasn't the day for it.

"You're the woman who landed the plane!" she exclaimed when I introduced myself. "That was wonderful, you saved Dean's life—everyone's life!" She seemed a little embarrassed at her enthusiasm. "I'm Lily Sawyer. Come in, Dean's resting, but I'll tell him you're here."

I walked into one of those low-ceiling living rooms so hidden from the sun that the lights have to be on all the time. Like living underground, in a bomb shelter. Beige furniture that belonged in a larger room was crowded in a horseshoe facing a small fireplace. On a cold winter night, it might have been okay. But this was a June morning, and I didn't even want to sit down. I perched on the arm of the heavy sofa.

Dean came down the stairs a moment later, followed by Lily. He was still in blue work shirt and jeans, looking pale but steady, and he nodded as he saw me.

"Would you like coffee?" Lily asked.

When I said I would, she slid past the sofa and through a narrow dining area to what had to be a cramped kitchen, behind the stairs.

"Glad I'm getting a chance to talk with you, O'Neal," Dean said, holding out his hand. I stood up and shook it. "To thank you, really. For saving my life."

We were both embarrassed.

"Hell, I had to save my own," I said, in my best macho tone.

He smiled and gestured me back toward the sofa, and I tried to get comfortable sitting on it, facing the fireplace, but it was too low and my legs were too long. I managed to stretch them out under the coffee table. He sat in a lounger just enough higher that his legs were okay.

"What knocked you out?" I asked.

"The coffee. Barbiturates in my thermos. Enough to kill me, if the hospital hadn't pumped my stomach." He smiled again, wryly. "Or if you hadn't landed the plane."

"Where'd you get the coffee?"

"From the kitchen of the Seraglio coffee shop. The same coffee everyone else drank. That's why I said barbiturates in the thermos—they couldn't have been in the coffee."

"Who had access to your thermos?"

"I'd say nobody, but that can't be true. I had stayed at the Seraglio the night before—I always do when I'm on an overnight at the lake—and in the morning I had breakfast, gave my thermos to the waitress and asked her to fill it, caught a ride on the Seraglio shuttle to the airport, stowed my gear in the cockpit, and did the walkaround. Then I poured a cup of coffee and went in to chat with Wynn Everett, the guy who runs Tahoe Aviation. That cup must have been all right. I didn't pour another cup until shortly before you arrived."

"The thermos was sitting in the cockpit? In plain sight?"

"Yeah, I guess so. But I didn't notice anyone near the plane."

"What about the flight attendant?"

"Stacy? She got there right before you did. I was afraid she wasn't going to make it, almost called the hotel."

Lily arrived with a tray holding three cups of coffee, cream, sugar, spoons, and napkins. She put the tray on the table, and I picked up a cup. Lily sat down in the chair across from Dean. She handed a cup to Dean and added cream to the remaining one.

"An act of faith," I said, taking a sip.

"I didn't dope my own coffee," he said stiffly.

"It was a cheap joke," I said, sorry I had made it. "I don't think you did. I don't think you're suicidal, and it wouldn't have occurred to you that I could land the plane."

"You're right."

"Besides, I don't think you were the target."

"No, I don't either. And I'll bet a carload of cops have already picked up Vince Marina's ex."

I put down the coffee cup. It was good coffee, but a little too hot.

"What do you know about that?"

"Only the rumors."

I waited. Lily edged forward in her chair, wanting to be in on whatever it was.

"I don't like repeating rumors," he added.

"If it makes you feel better, Vince has hired me to check into this."

"Then he's already told you."

We were eye to eye, like a kid's game of stare-down.

"I haven't asked him about the rumors. He may not know the rumors."

Dean blinked.

"The rumor is his ex-wife is trying to kill him. He has to know that."

"How? Why?"

"The answer to how is with a knife or a truck or whatever's at hand. I'm not sure about why. The story, as it is circulating, is that they had one of those show-business Catholic marriages, where she raised the three kids and he did whatever he pleased. Two years ago—after thirty years of marriage—he told her he wanted a divorce. She went nuts. He arranged his schedule so that he could spend some time in Nevada, and filed here. He had already established residence here for tax purposes—I think he has some deal with the Seraglio about that—so nobody gave him a bad time. I don't know how the attorneys got her to sign the papers. They probably threatened to skin her poodle alive or something—don't quote me, I don't know. But she signed."

"Did she get screwed on the deal?"

"Who knows? I don't think she has to sell lingerie at Weinstock's, if that's what you mean."

"Is there another woman?"

"Vince Marina likes women, he always has. I don't know if there's one you could call 'another' woman."

"Do you fly him around a lot? Would you know?"

Dean shook his head.

"The Seraglio jet is available to him, but I wouldn't say he's abused the privilege. I'll sometimes pick him up in L.A., fly him to Vegas or the lake, usually with Benny Elcano, sometimes with one or two of his kids, never with a bimbo. And sure, there could be a woman I didn't know about. I've told you, we're talking rumors here."

"Are there any women around the Seraglio who were around Vince a lot and might be willing to talk about it?"

He had to think about that one.

"Rita Mason. Twenty-one dealer, swing shift. And Demetria Jones. Did you see the show?"

I nodded.

"She's the first dead Indian."

"Thanks."

"You're welcome."

I picked up my coffee cup and took a couple of sips in succession. I hated leaving it, but couldn't think of anything more to ask. Well, maybe one question.

"Can you think of any way Vince Marina's ex-wife could have doped your coffee?"

"As far as I know, she isn't even at the lake. But it ought to be easy to check."

"Yeah, right. She's fairly well-known up there, isn't she? Wouldn't she be recognized at the airport?"

"If she was seen, yeah. What's bothering you?"

"The other attempts—at least as far as I've heard about them—were straightforward. This one was devious and complicated. I have to wonder if someone isn't trying to cash in on the rumors."

Sawyer shook his head.

"I know you want to earn whatever Vince's paying you, but my money's on the wife."

I took a couple more fast sips and said good-bye, shaking hands all around and fending off Lily Sawyer's gratitude.

Finding my way out of the complex back to my Mustang— a dark green, rebuilt, 1968 classic—was a little easier than finding the condo, although I wished I had left a trail of crumbs.

There was nothing more I could do in Reno, so I picked up Interstate 80, turned south on 395, and headed for the Mount Rose highway and the lake. After calling Deke, I had thrown a pair of jeans, a couple of shirts, a couple of changes of underwear, a robe, and bathroom stuff into a canvas flight bag and stuck it in the trunk. I was close enough to home that I could always drive down if I needed something. Or I could buy it, on what Vince Marina was paying me.

Driving down through Carson City and picking up 50 would have been flatter and faster than going to South Shore, but less scenic. I liked the slow climb through pine trees, the sudden blast of afternoon sun reflected from the lake as the highway dipped beyond the summit, the curving crawl around the water, through the acres of pines, and back to the water. The marvel, really, was not that the lake was messed up in places, but that so much of it was still untouched.

I was still early enough that I didn't need to stop at the Zephyr Cove house yet. Instead, I inched through the traffic at the state border, parked at the Tahoe Valley airport, and walked past the main terminal to the smaller Tahoe Aviation building.

Wynn Everett had a glass eye. That was the first thing I noticed, that his right eye was larger than his left and had the sightless stare of a glass eye. The color match was good, though. Light brown. Personally, I think I'd choose a patch. He was tall, maybe sixty, with flying gray hair and a narrow nose that pointed at his chin. He stood up when I walked into the small office, and held out his hand when I introduced myself.

"I heard about what you did, Miss O'Neal," he said, "and I'd be proud to buy you a drink sometime."

"Thanks," I said, taking his hand and looking at his good eye. "I'd be very pleased to accept."

"What can I do to help you today?"

"I'm trying to figure out what might have happened, who might have doped Dean Sawyer's thermos."

"I wish I could help." He shook his head. "I'm afraid I just didn't see anybody that morning, nobody except Dean, and then Stacy, and the four of you that got into the plane. I'm sorry."

"No maintenance people? No plane owners?"

"Nope. It was real quiet. An American flight landed and took off again, but nothing down here."

"Could someone have gotten past you and Dean to the plane?"

"Someone who knew where the plane was and where we were, sure. Somebody could have walked through the gates and snuck around the building to where the plane was."

"You thought about it, didn't you?"

He smiled and winked his good eye at me.

"You betcha. There're gonna be a bunch of people besides you asking that question, and I've walked all over this airport and thought it out."

"So you're telling me it had to be someone who knew the plane, the airport, Dean, and figured he'd have a thermos."

He nodded.

"I figure it's somebody who flew with him before."

"Any ideas?"

He laughed, openmouthed. His right teeth were different from his left, too. A little whiter and straighter. I looked for signs of scarring, but whoever had put his face back together had done a good job. All I could tell was that the smile was a little wider on the left than the right.

"Not me. I don't know nothin' about it."

"How about Connie Marina?"

"Could be—could be anybody, I guess. But I didn't see her. Or anyone else."

"And you would have recognized her."

"Sure would. So I guess I can't help you."

"Yeah, right. Well, if you wake up in the middle of the night and you can't sleep because something just hit you, call and tell me about it." I pulled a business card out of my jeans pocket and gave it to him. "I'll be staying at the Seraglio guest house for the next few days, but if you don't want to call me there, just leave a message on the machine."

I turned and started out the door.

"Miss O'Neal?"

I stopped, but didn't look at him.

"I'd still like to buy you that drink, Miss O'Neal."

I glanced back, but the lopsided smile now looked like a leer to me, so I left.

Vince Marina had discussed his food schedule when performing during the interview with Sandra—a main meal at noon, a light supper about seven, and an even lighter snack about two in the morning, when he was unwinding after the midnight show. It wasn't quite six when I knocked on the door of the guest house. Guest mansion was more like it.

Benny Elcano opened the door. He smiled his anxious, furrowed smile.

"Good to see you, honey. Come on in. I'll show you to your room—you've got about an hour before we eat, but come on down to the living room for a drink whenever you want."

I followed him to the left and up the stairs. He opened the first door we came to, exposing a room just large enough for a double bed and a hotel-style squat dresser that sat next to a small closet.

"This is yours," he said. "The bathroom is two doors down, on the left."

"What's the rest of the layout?"

"Oh—the next door is mine—we share the bathroom— and at the end of the hall is the master bedroom. Vince has that, and his own bathroom. Masaka—I think you met him last time you were here—has his quarters on the ground floor, near the kitchen."

"And we're the only ones staying here?"

"Well, yeah. But Tommy Durant, Vince's accompanist, sometimes eats with us. He could stay here, but he's staying at the Seraglio."

"Why?"

Benny made a dice-rolling motion with his hand.

"He has a habit and likes to be close. When his debts pile up, Vince talks to the Seraglio. Otherwise, Tommy'd be dead by now."

"Will he be here tonight?"

"Yeah, he's downstairs with Vince now."

I nodded.

"Okay. I'll be down in a few minutes."

Benny sort of backed out of the door, shutting it behind him.

I tossed my bag on the bed and checked my appearance in the mirror over the dresser. I had to bend my knees a little to get the top of my head in. The western-style blue shirt I was wearing with my jeans would do just fine. Bodyguards don't have to dress.

I walked down the hall to the shared bathroom to wash my face. Benny had left his shaving stuff lying out, and I had a sudden ugly glimpse of what living with someone was like. I brushed my hair back into its usual nape-of-the-neck ponytail and decided I was ready to go down the stairs to the living room.

Vince was standing where I had first seen him, looking out the glass doors onto the patio, a drink in one hand and a cigarette in the other, this time wearing a gray polo shirt and slacks. Benny was sitting in one of the brocade chairs, also holding a drink. A third man, thin, sixtyish, showing a fringe of white hair below a Dodgers cap, was sitting on the couch. Nothing seemed to be happening. I didn't feel as if I was interrupting anything, like a conversation. It was as if they had been together so long they were frozen in amber.

"Hi," I said from the archway.

Benny jumped up.

"Yeah, Freddie, this is Tommy Durant."

The man on the couch nodded. Pretty men don't age well.

They end up looking soft and weak. I was certain Tommy Durant had once been pretty.

"You want a drink?" Benny asked.

"Sure, I'll take a beer."

He walked over to the wet bar and opened a small refrigerator.

"We got Corona, Heineken, and Bud."

"Bud's fine."

Vince still hadn't turned.

"Mr. Marina," I began.

"Vince."

"Vince. We need to talk about just what it is you want from me."

"After the show," he said. "We can talk after the show. In the meantime, have dinner, enjoy yourself."

Benny handed me the beer. I took it over to the other brocade chair, sat, and waited. I wasn't having fun yet.

"Could we talk about what happened yesterday?" I asked, when it appeared no one else would start anything.

"After the show," he said.

"You know, you're a pretty impressive pilot," Benny volunteered. "Where'd you learn to fly like that?"

Benny was squirming in his chair. Vince might be calm about attempts on his life, but Benny clearly didn't like it that the latest one had included him as well. As I looked at the two of them it occurred to me that I was a compromise. Benny wanted a bodyguard, Vince didn't. I was something in between.

"One year my mother told me I could have anything I wanted for my birthday," I said. "I asked for flying lessons. The rest happened over time."

"Yeah, that's great." Benny tried to think of a follow-up question but couldn't.

Tommy was playing a personal tune with his fingers on the coffee table. Vince stared out the window.

"Hey, Vince," Tommy said suddenly. "I got an idea. Why not add a medley of old songs to the act? Really old songs. 'Sweet Sixteen.' 'When You and I Were Young.' Maybe even some Stephen Foster stuff, like 'I Dream of

Jeannie.' The Reno crowd'll love it. What do you think?''

Vince nodded.

"Work it out, Tommy. Sounds good.''

"You wanta eat now?''

We all jumped. No one had heard Masaka come in. He stood in the doorway, short, maybe in his late twenties, wearing a white cook's jacket. His black hair was moussed into spikes, and I wondered what he did on his night off.

We followed him over to the dining area, where the long table had been set for four. Vince sat at the head, Benny and Tommy on either side. I sat next to Benny.

We ate our salads in silence, and nobody could get a conversation going during the main course, which consisted of a small fat steak sitting on a piece of toast, with some spoonfuls of almost raw vegetables. Nobody meant Benny. The rest of us didn't try. Dessert was a scoop of peach ice cream with a fresh chocolate-chip cookie stuck in it. We all had coffee, even Vince. I was sort of betting he'd pass.

The car and driver were waiting when we were finished. The driver still seemed anonymous to me—partly because no one had bothered to introduce us—but I knew I was going to have to talk to him at some point. Benny rode in front, Tommy, Vince, and I in the back. Vince sat in the middle. I scrunched as close to the door as I could, not comfortable with the contact. We all got out at the artists' entrance.

I went with them to Vince's dressing room, but short of tasting every open bottle on the bar for poison, there didn't seem much I could do. Anyway, Vince had to change. Benny assured me that my name was with the maître d' so that I could walk in to the show at the last minute and sit at Vince's reserved table.

I wandered out to the casino.

Casinos always look red to me. The red carpets and the red walls vibrate, emitting their own light through a constant smoky haze, as if the doorway to the Inferno were in the basement. Some psychologist probably told a casino designer that red inflames the senses, makes impulses uncontrollable, and every casino from then on was painted red.

The Seraglio casino was a dark red smoky expanse about the size of Candlestick Park. Not all of it was red, of course. The covers of the craps and roulette tables were green, and the flashing lights on the slot machines came in many colors, although red predominated. I threaded through the maze of machines and tables to a centrally located cage with CHANGE in red neon letters hanging above it.

I waited until the short, nervous man in front of me and the heavyset woman in front of him had been supplied with quarters, and then stepped to the window.

"Where could I find a twenty-one dealer named Rita Mason?"

"The pit just this side of the coffee shop," said a man whose white shirt and black vest identified him as an employee as much as the badge he was wearing.

I started to say thanks, but he was looking past me to the next paying customer. I should have asked him where the coffee shop was. But I figured it was toward the rear, and I was right.

There were six twenty-one tables in a ring separated by just a couple of rows of slot machines from the coffee-shop entrance. Only one of the dealers could be Rita Mason. Four of the other five were men, and the one other woman was too old and too tired. Rita Mason was maybe thirty, with short blond hair and smooth skin. I moved to a slot machine where I could watch to see when she went on a break. I fished in my pocket for quarters, found only two, and flicked on the machine's change light.

A woman who looked so young I would have checked her ID before serving appeared next to me. Most of her outfit was high heels and apron. I got a five-dollar roll that I planned to charge to expenses and began slowly dropping them in one of the slots and pulling the handle. You couldn't win very much on a single quarter—the machine improved the payout as you dropped up to five quarters on one pull—but you couldn't lose very fast, either. The bars, the plums, and the blanks clanked slowly around on their independent reels. Some technologies never change. I still had a few quarters left when Rita slapped her hands on the table to show she wasn't walking off with anything and turned toward the coffee shop.

I caught up with her at the entrance.

"Do you mind if I join you?"

"Yes," she said calmly, fixing me with the solid blue-eyed gaze of a woman who had been taking care of herself for a long time. Her chin was a little too square and her stance a little too tough for classic beauty. She was short, maybe five-four, but she stood like a tall woman.

I pulled out my ID.

"Somebody has been trying to kill Vince Marina, and he's hired me to look into it."

She coughed out a short laugh.

"Vince hired a woman? Okay, I got a short break and I need to eat. Come on."

She nodded to the hostess and we sat in a red leather booth that could have been in the coffee shop of any casino in the state. Wake up in a casino coffee shop with amnesia and you'd have to look at a matchbook cover to know where you were.

Rita caught the eye of our waitress, exchanged a greeting, and ordered a club sandwich and coffee. I ordered a beer. I resisted an impulse to flag the Keno runner.

"What do you want to know?" she asked.

"First, why weren't you surprised when I said someone was trying to kill Vince Marina?"

She shrugged.

"Everybody has heard his ex-wife is trying to kill him."

"How has everybody heard that?"

"I don't know—I don't know how to trace the story back for you. This is a small community, and once a rumor like that starts, it bounces off the walls like an echo."

"What's the rumor about yesterday?"

"Just that Vince left in a jet and came back in a car. Plane trouble."

"Yeah, okay, that's close enough. How about telling me where you were yesterday morning, between, say, ten and noon?"

"I have no alibi. I slept until a little after ten, fixed myself

some breakfast, walked down to the beach. I live with a
roommate, but she didn't come home last night, and nobody
who knows me saw me until I came to work at four
o'clock.'' She paused, looked down, then looked purposefully back at me and continued. ''Why are you talking to
me? Whatever happened yesterday, you should be asking
Connie Marina about it, not me.''

The waitress deftly slid the club sandwich with its heap of
potato salad in the middle of four toothpicked quarters onto
the table. We both looked at her and smiled, and the coffee
and beer followed.

''So why are you talking to me?'' she asked again as she
picked up one of the sandwich quarters and removed its
toothpick.

''I'm trying to get a line on why Vince's ex-wife might
be after his head.''

''And somebody told you it might be because of me?
That's a joke, right?''

''Not quite that.''

She put the sandwich down and pushed the plate away.

''What did you hear?''

''Just that you'd hung out with him. That's all.''

''I think I just lost my appetite.''

''Well, you know what you said about a small community, about rumors like echos.''

I felt bad saying that. But she just shrugged again.

''I had an affair with Vince. I happened to be the woman
he was sleeping with when he served the divorce papers on
his wife. But as it turned out, it was just a coincidence. I
could have been anyone.''

''Did you want to kill him?''

''No. I wanted to kill me.'' She riveted her eyes into
mine. ''I was going to drive my car off the road, I was
driving down Mount Rose at eighty, heading for a curve,
and I swore I was going straight off, but my dog was with
me, and I couldn't kill her. Anything else? I gotta get back
to work.''

''Nothing. I'm sorry.''

''Yeah, okay, you pay for the sandwich.''

She stalked out. I sat there and finished my beer.

"Was something wrong with the sandwich?" the waitress asked. She was young and worried, as if it might be her mistake, and Rita was a regular.

"No. Rita just misjudged her time. Pack the sandwich in a doggy bag and save it. She might want it later."

I hoped Rita would want it later.

By the time I got over to the showroom, the cowboys were already shooting the Indians. I had planned on spotting Demetria Jones and catching her between shows, but I wasn't sure I was up for another conversation. I was still standing at the back deciding when the chorus number ended and the single spot went up on Vince. Then I heard the first notes of "I'm a Fool to Want You," in that low boozy, perfect voice, and I thought of Rita, and I had to leave. Backstage was as good as anywhere.

The dancers had a couple of hours before they went on again, and as I reached the stage door they were scattering. Some—mostly Indians—had changed, some—mostly cowboys—had thrown jackets over their costumes. All still wore exotic makeup, the heavy pancake and dark eyeliner of opera. The Seraglio dinner theater probably was, as I thought about it, bigger than most legit houses. I don't know about the Met, because I've never been there.

I grabbed an Egyptian-eyed cowboy by the arm.

"Demetria Jones," I said.

He looked wildly around.

"I think she's still inside. Ask at the door."

The man at the door, a burly fellow who looked as if he should have been Vince Marina's bodyguard, remembered me. He confirmed that Demetria Jones was still inside and pointed me toward the dancers' dressing room. I started toward it, but stopped when I heard Benny's voice, raised and anxious, coming from the opposite direction.

"No," he was saying. "You can't wait in his dressing room. Demetria, he knows where to find you. When he wants to see you, he will. This isn't a good night for a confrontation, you gotta trust me on this one."

"Benny, you get the fuck out of my way or I'll make a scene in the hall when he comes off stage."

She was tall, long-legged, still in her fringed, Indian bikini, and the color of extra-rich gourmet coffee ice cream. All over. Wide, frantic, black eyes dominated an exotic face. Wiry black curls were fighting to escape the confines of the Pocahontas braids trailing down her back. I walked up and took her arm.

She jumped.

"Who the fuck are you?"

"I'm Vince's bodyguard, and I think we ought to talk."

"Vince's bodyguard? You're his bodyguard? What the hell does that mean? Is bodyguard a new word for it? I don't believe it, you're not even pretty."

"Yeah, and you won't be either, unless you come with me right now."

I stared straight at her—she was only an inch or so shorter than I am—and she broke. It was a bluff, of course. I couldn't have roughed her if she'd called it. But she was impressed, and so was Benny.

I steered her back to the dancers' dressing room, threw the door open, and slammed it against the wall. No sense backing down at that point. Two bikinied Indians sharing a joint tried to focus their dilated pupils in horror.

"Grab your coat," I said. "We're going outside."

She pulled a trench coat off a long rack, the kind you find full of cheap clothes in discount stores, put it on, and belted it. I took her arm again and steered her outside, nodding at the doorman as we passed. I worked our way out into the parking lot. She stopped.

"I'm still wearing dance slippers," she said, leaning against a black Lincoln. "I don't want to ruin them."

I dropped her arm.

"Okay. We'll talk here. Why did you want to see Vince?"

She laughed, sadly.

"Why? Because I heard he's in trouble, and I need to know he's okay. Because he doesn't want to talk to me.

Because I don't believe it's over. Why. Why did you want to stop me?''

"I'm not stopping you. Right now I want to talk to you. And I guess I think it's part of my job to keep you from embarrassing him in public. But I got no problem if you want to talk to him.''

The parking lot was on a slope that led to a stand of pines, but it was high enough that we could see the lake beyond. We both stared out at the water. The lights from the hotel illuminated the first row of trees, and beyond that the trees were a massive presence in the darkness, and then there were just the tips of the waves, reflecting starlight. I shivered. I had left my jacket in Vince's dressing room, and I needed it now.

"What do you want to talk to me about?''

"There've been some attempts on Vince's life.''

"And you wanted to talk to me? It's his ex-wife, Connie. Talk to her. Everybody knows it's Connie who wants to kill him.''

"Not you. You don't want to kill him.''

She slumped down, still flat-footed, head to her knees, in a position only a dancer could hold.

"I don't know. Maybe I do.''

"You want to tell me about it?''

She shook her head without losing her balance.

I wanted to comfort her in some way, but I couldn't come up with anything to offer.

"I was worried about him,'' she finally said. "I haven't tried to kill him. I just want to talk to him, that's all. I need to talk to him.''

"Okay. Look, don't try to talk to him tonight. Benny's right, the timing isn't good. Let me try to set something up. I'll talk to Vince.''

She stood up and looked at me.

"You really don't have anything going with him, do you?''

"No. I really don't.''

She stuck her hands in her sleeves, hugging herself.

"I gotta go. I only have a two-hour break.''

I watched her walk away, through the parking lot, not toward the stage door. My stomach was churning and my heart was pounding.

I needed someplace quiet to sit for a moment, and I thought Vince's dressing room might be clear. It was, except for his piped-in voice. He was about halfway through his act. "Win or lose, I'm a moonlight gambler," he crooned. Gambler, hell. He was the house—the odds were with him all the way. I decided what I was going to say in my conversation with Vince Marina: I quit.

I held on to that thought all through the second show, even as he sang a retrospective of his thirty-year career. I held on to it easily as the hangers-on flooded his dressing room, ate his buffet, and drank his booze—or the Seraglio's, whatever. I wrapped it around me all the ride to the house, not letting any part of my body touch him.

As we walked in the front door he said, "Meet me in the living room, honey. I'll be down in a minute."

The living room was dark, except for the low moon reflecting off the pale sand and the tips of the waves through the glass doors, and I didn't turn on any lights. I sat in one of the brocade chairs and waited.

When Vince came down the stairs about ten minutes later, he had replaced the tux he wore for the show with a dark silk dressing gown. He didn't turn on any lights either. He walked to the bar, fixed himself a drink, and moved to what was apparently his usual spot, staring out at the lake. He put the glass down on a low table and lit a cigarette.

"If your ex-wife doesn't kill you, those things will," I said.

He turned, startled.

"I didn't see you sitting there. I thought you weren't here."

I didn't say anything. Vince picked up his glass and looked out toward the lake again.

When it became clear he had forgotten my presence, I said, "I quit."

"Okay," he said.

And then I couldn't let it go at that.

"Why did you want to hire me, anyway? Just to make Benny happy?"

"No. Not just that. I thought maybe you could talk to Connie."

"And find out why she's trying to kill you?"

He shrugged.

"If you want to. You're right, I hired you for Benny. I wouldn't have hired someone as long as Connie was only trying to kill me. If she wants to badly enough, she'll find a way to do it. I hired you because the plane crash would have taken me, Benny, you, and three other people. Somebody smart and sensible has to tell her that's no good, I'm the one she's mad at, not the people who happen to be around me. I thought you might be able to do that."

"Why is she mad at you?"

"I don't know, honey." He sighed. "I really don't. A woman wants something from you, something you don't have inside you to give, and then she gets mad when you don't give it."

Shit. I understood that.

"What did she do—when she tried to kill you?" I asked, finally, when I had to break the silence.

He sighed again, as if it was a long story and he didn't want to tell it.

"The first time was a week or so after I had told her I was filing for divorce. I went to the L.A. house to pick up a few things, and she came at me with a knife. I thought it was just the anger of the moment, I thought she'd get over it." He paused for a sip of his drink. "The next time I went to the house, I made sure she wasn't there. She came back as I was leaving, though, and drove up on the curb trying to hit me."

He sipped again, and this time the pause was so long I thought maybe he was through. But he wasn't.

"When the divorce papers had been signed, she rented a truck, threw all the rest of the things I had at the L.A. house into the back of it, drove to the town house I'd bought, and dumped the stuff in the middle of the street. I came out to see what was going on, I thought maybe I could talk to her, and she tried to run me down."

Another long pause.

"That's it?"

He nodded.

"Those sound like spontaneous acts of passion to me," I said. "Drugging Sawyer's coffee, on the other hand, was premeditated. Not the same MO. Are you sure nobody else is trying to kill you?"

"Not that I know of, honey."

I was getting nervous, talking with him in the dark. I could barely see his face, and I wanted to know what he was thinking.

"Do you mind if I turn on a light?"

"Yes, I do. Lights wake me up. One night I opened the refrigerator door and sang three songs to the butter dish."

The line caught me off guard, and I laughed. Vince turned and smiled at me for the first time. I stopped laughing. I didn't want to like him.

"Okay, I won't quit until I've talked with Connie," I said, as sternly as I could. "Where is she now?"

"I don't know. She got two houses in the divorce, one in L.A. and one here, at Crystal Bay."

"So you don't even know if she was around yesterday."

"No."

"Have you talked to the police?"

"If you mean about what happened yesterday, as far as I know, nobody reported it. If you're asking about earlier attempts, the answer is no. No police."

I thought about whether someone other than those of us immediately involved would report the barbiturates in Dean Sawyer's coffee to the police. I wasn't sure if this was something Washoe Medical personnel would be compelled to report, or if they could be persuaded not to. If it was what Vince wanted, Benny would certainly try to do the persuading. After all, Dean was okay, and accidents happen. The airport would have to report it to the FAA, but if all it said was "sick pilot," the papers might end up in a file somewhere, never investigated.

"You could get an injunction to keep her away from you, you know that."

He shrugged again.

"I could. I don't know what good it would do. And I don't want to do that, I don't want to bring the police in. I just want her to go ahead and live her life without me."

"And you can't figure out why she won't do that."

Vince turned away again, back to the lake.

"Yeah, that's right."

"Vince? I'll talk with Connie for you. But there's somebody I can't talk to for you."

"What?"

"Demetria Jones wants to see you."

He looked puzzled. I could see that even in the dim, reflected light. For a minute, I was afraid he couldn't remember who she was. My stomach knotted again.

"Demetria? Isn't she all right? I told them they couldn't fire her, I didn't care how much she yelled in the dressing room."

"It's not her job, Vince. It's you. She's worried about you. She wants to know you're all right."

One tear formed in his right eye, inched over his cheekbone, and slid to his jaw, its passage shimmering in the moonlight. Then it disappeared.

"You tell her I'm all right," he said.

"She wants to hear it from you."

"Oh, God."

He lurched toward me and fell to his knees. His head landed in my lap. I froze.

"I just need to be close to somebody," he sobbed. "Please, honey, I just need somebody to hold me."

I couldn't move. I couldn't touch him. He kept sobbing against my thigh. His after-shave smelled too sweet, as if it was covering up something sour underneath.

"Not me, Vince. Whatever it is you need, I just don't have it to give."

He stayed there a moment longer. Finally he straightened up.

"Benny can give you the address in Crystal Bay. And the L.A. address, if you need it."

"Okay. I'll take care of it tomorrow."

I had begun to think he had an unlimited tolerance for whatever it was he drank, but there was a noticeable weave as he climbed the stairs. I stayed where I was until I was certain he had reached his own bedroom.

And when I reached mine, I shoved a chair under the doorknob, just in case.

Chapter

3

NO ONE DISTURBED my sleep—once I succumbed to it—by rattling the knob. And there was no sign of either Vince or Benny when I got up in the morning. From the look of our shared bathroom, Benny hadn't been there since the night before.

I washed, dressed, and went downstairs. The sideboard held an urn of coffee, a pitcher of orange juice on ice, a plate of assorted pastry, a bowl of apples, a few individual cereal boxes, and all the necessary dishes and silver. I poured myself coffee and juice, chose a Danish with apples, nuts, and frosting on it, and looked for a place to sit and eat. I would have been embarrassed, all by myself at the long table. I balanced the juice on the plate with the Danish and walked out onto the deck.

It was still early enough that the shadows stretched across the wood and darkened the sand. The day was picture-postcard perfect, the water light blue and clear, the green trees and snowcapped purple mountains on the other side stark against a sky so translucent that you had to believe it was the true color of space. Snowcapped. That's what Nevada means. But those mountains were on the other side of the lake, in California, and they still had snow in June, just like the ones on this side. Funny how arbitrary borders are.

I found two cushioned chairs with wide wooden arms hidden so that they wouldn't spoil the view from the open glass doors. I sat in one and put the plate, glass, and mug on the table between them. Probably it was for moments like this that I had kept going to camp all those years, facing the humiliation of an inability to control large, clumsy hands that became all thumbs when ordered to etch a pattern on leather for a wallet that no one would ever use. Because the lake had always been this beautiful, this peaceful, and I was sorry that I had waited so long before coming back to remember that.

When I had finished with the juice and Danish, I took the plate and glass inside and refilled my coffee. I wasn't sure what to do next. I was saved from indolence when Benny came down the stairs.

"Hi, honey, how ya doing?"

He poured a cup of coffee and inspected the pastries.

"Fine. Vince said you'd give me Connie's address in Crystal Bay."

I was getting really tired of men who called me honey.

"Yeah, sure."

He described the house and how to get there as he placed two sticky buns on a plate and moved them to the table. I knew the area and was sure I could find it.

"Don't you want to call first—see if she's there?" he asked.

"No. I like to surprise people."

I didn't want to spend any more time with Benny than I had to, so I regretfully left half of my second cup of coffee. My Mustang was still out in front, but someone had washed and waxed it during the night. It hadn't looked that good since I had had it painted and the bodywork done at the same time I had the engine rebuilt. Usually it just looked like an old car. For once, it looked like a classic. I should do that myself occasionally, wash and wax it.

I turned north out of the private drive onto Route 50 and drove slowly back the way I had come the day before, past the Mount Rose highway, almost to the northern state line. The differences between the north and south ends of Lake Tahoe mirrored the differences between the north and south ends of the state. South Shore was big and crowded and flashy, and all the money was new and slithery, as if it couldn't stay in any one hand for too long. North Shore was cooler and older and expected to keep its money for a long time.

When the first big casino at the north end was built, just west of Crystal Bay, the minimum bet at the cheapest tables was five dollars. And that was in the fifties, when five dollars bought more than a hamburger and a cup of coffee. The story was that the man who had taken the order for the napkins and matchbooks and all the other stuff with the club's logo had called to make a reservation for the opening night, wanting to join the celebration. He was told bluntly that they didn't want his business. He just wasn't chic enough—he'd clash with the decor. Of course, the club ultimately had to back down—there really weren't that many high rollers at Lake Tahoe, especially at the genteel north end, and even more especially after the Nevada Gaming Commission revoked the gambling licenses of a couple of the partners because of their alleged underworld connections. Pretty soon the bet at the cheap tables was down to a dollar. Still a long way from the quarter tables—or worse, the dime tables—in the more sordid corners of downtown Reno.

Even the pine trees at the north end of the lake seemed haughtier. The one real blot on the landscape was the Ponderosa Ranch, created as the setting for a television series, now a tourist attraction. I always look the other way when I drive by.

The house I was looking for wasn't actually in Crystal Bay, of course. It was off a private road about a mile beyond, a road that took three nasty turns to discourage casual callers before becoming a driveway.

Connie Marina's house was what you'd expect a Lake Tahoe cabin to be, if you could afford any Lake Tahoe cabin you wanted. The outside was cedar logs, varnished to a high gloss. There was a tall roof on the central part of the building and a two-story wing on either side. Just your average half-a-million-dollar vacation home.

I parked next to a baby-blue Cadillac, one of the ugly

small ones, with a California plate. The big ones are ugly, too, but the small ones win the tarnished ring for ugly. At least someone was home. I crunched across the gravel and knocked on the front door.

The woman who opened the door was short and bloated, but she carried herself with confidence in the beauty that she probably once had. Her skin was porcelain, and at a guess had been taken up once, because her cheeks were round and full but her chin line didn't look bad. Her blond hair had been expensively shaded and shagged, her gray-green extra-large sweats didn't come from a discount store, and her sharp blue eyes stabbed me from behind the kind of muted makeup that only rich women wear well.

"Connie Marina?" I asked, when she didn't say anything.

"Yes."

There was an implied criticism of my existence in the way she dropped the word.

"I'm Freddie O'Neal." I pulled out the card case with my ID and handed it to her. "I'd like to speak with you a moment."

"About what?" She handed it back.

"About the attempts on Vince Marina's life. Especially the last one, which could have taken a half-dozen other people, too."

"I don't know what you're talking about, taking other people, too."

There was gravel in her voice.

"Then maybe you'll let me come in and explain."

She thought about it, still pinning me with her electric-blue eyes. Given my boots and her Reeboks, I was almost a foot taller. I think she got tired of looking up.

"Okay, come on in."

I followed her into a large cedar-paneled room with a spectacular view of pine trees and the lake. The room had a cathedral ceiling cut by an open loft. A massive stone fireplace in the center of the room doubtless had a secondary hearth in the loft, but all in all the room looked like a real energy waster and a bitch to heat. But beautiful. Heaven, if you could afford it.

The furniture was covered in an imitation Indian pattern executed in strange pastels, but the rug on the hardwood floor looked real. There was a wet bar in one corner with a man leaning against it. He was tall, white-haired, with the kind of looks you'd call stately, like Lloyd Bentsen, and he had a glass in his hand. Sometimes the habit of hanging out with men who drink is hard to break.

"David, this is Freddie O'Neal," Connie said. "She's a private eye. Vince hired her."

"Why?"

"Because I tried to kill him. Why else?"

David shrugged.

"Freddie, this is David Troy. He's a friend."

I nodded at David to acknowledge the introduction, and he nodded back. Connie gestured toward the couch and I sat. She sat in one of the low armchairs nearby. David stayed at the bar.

"So," she said. "What did he tell you to tell me?"

"You do admit you've tried to kill him?" I countered.

"Yeah, sure I admit it. No point in denying it—Benny Elcano was standing on the sidewalk hopping up and down and yelling at me the last time." She laughed, a low, gravelly laugh. "Ah, God, it was great. You should have seen Vince running down the street, dodging the truck. I would have done it. I could feel it, how the bumper was going to catch him behind the knees and knock him to the pavement, the crunch of bone as the tires passed over his body and the weight of the truck fell upon his spine. I could see his crushed, bloody corpse lying in the street. But he squeezed between two parked cars, and I couldn't get him. I have dreams about an open field. Just me, Vince, and the truck."

"Why?"

"Why did I try to kill him?"

I nodded. She seemed a little surprised that I had interrupted her reverie on murder.

"Oh, hell, honey, you're too young to understand."

I could get tired of women who called me honey, too.

"Try me."

"I gave Vince my life, and he threw it away."

"So take it back."

"That's what I was doing, taking my life back." She leaned forward in her chair, blue eyes narrowed to a spot between intensity and madness. "That was gonna give it back to me, that was gonna tell him how wrong he was, all those years, when he was the one who counted, not me, when this whole family revolved around him, when nobody mattered but him, when nothing was important but what he wanted, so that when he walked out, there wasn't anything important left. He was gonna know how he was wrong by dying. And I was still gonna be alive. I was gonna be alive and he was gonna be dead. That's how I was taking my life back."

"Can't you just pretend he's dead?"

The gravelly laugh again.

"No. He controls my life, honey, just the way he always did. He bought my lawyer, the one I hired for the divorce, he bought him away from me, so the divorce settlement says he can cut me off with no alimony anytime he wants to. I'm middle-aged and fat and I've never worked a day in my life, except raising kids and taking care of him. And he can cut off the alimony if he gets unhappy."

"Jesus. If trying to run him down with a truck doesn't make him unhappy, what would?"

"That's not the point!" she shouted.

"Okay, I know. All right, suppose he cut you off. You got two houses in the settlement. Couldn't you just sell one? Start over on the proceeds?"

"How much would I have after taxes? I'd be living on nothing while he'd be living big! Rubbing my face in it, every time I saw his name in the papers!"

"Isn't there something you want to do with your life besides hate him?"

That caught her. She slumped in her chair and hugged herself, a gesture that reminded me sadly of Demetria Jones.

"No. There's nothing I want to do with my life besides hate him."

David Troy walked over and sat down on the arm of Connie's chair. She leaned against him, and he patted her shoulder. I waited for her to regain control.

"You've told me about the truck incident," I finally said. "My guess is you wouldn't deny two others, the kitchen knife and the car." She didn't move. "What about the barbiturates in Dean Sawyer's coffee?"

"What do you mean?" she asked, straightening up.

"You know Dean Sawyer, right?"

"Yeah, sure, the Seraglio pilot."

"Somebody doped Sawyer's coffee, which would not only have taken out Vince, but the other passengers on the Seraglio plane as well."

"Not me, honey." She shook her head decisively. "Whatever Vince is doing, he can't hang that one on me. I want him dead, and there were a couple of moments when I thought I was going to be there to make it happen, but it was just the two of us. I don't know anything about Dean's coffee or the Seraglio plane."

"Can you think of someone else who might want him dead—and not care who goes with him?"

"Look at his life. There's probably a hundred of them."

"What about you?" I asked, turning to David Troy.

He paused before answering, slightly startled at being included, then slowly shook his head.

"I have no problem with Vince," he said, with a barely perceptible slur in his voice. "I've only met him twice, and he's always been polite to me."

"Look, honey, neither of us knows anything about doping Dean's coffee. But if Vince thinks I'm plotting to take him out, that's okay. So why don't you go back to him and tell him that one of these days I'm gonna get him. I don't know when or how, but when I'm ready, he won't be able to stop me. Yeah, let him think about that for a while."

Connie leaned away from David, obviously pleased with the idea that Vince might be afraid of her.

"I'll tell him."

I drove straight back to the Seraglio guest house. I was even more certain now that I had talked with her that Connie Marina hadn't doped the coffee, hadn't planned the crash. If she doped coffee, it would be Vince's, it would be spur of the moment, and she'd be sitting there watching him drink it. No long-distance stuff for her.

The gold limo was parked in front of the door. I pulled up and parked behind it. When I got out, I could see the driver, polishing the hood with a chamois cloth.

"Hey, that's what you did to the Mustang! Thanks." I walked up and held out my hand. "I'm Freddie O'Neal."

"I'm Andrew," he said, ignoring my hand and continuing to polish. "You have a nice car, Miss O'Neal. Takes a real pretty shine."

"Yes, well, thanks again." I clumsily retracted my hand. "Andrew, you remember the morning you drove us to the airport—the morning we had the plane trouble?" He didn't say anything, so I continued. "Was there anybody hanging around after we took off?"

He kept polishing. He was a small man, bald, wearing rimless glasses, and I couldn't find a distinguishing feature. I knew I'd have trouble recognizing him if he weren't wearing his undertaker-black suit.

"No," he said, finally, when I was starting to fidget in the silence, "I didn't even see Wynn. Wynn's who you should ask—Wynn Everett. He's always there."

I wondered what he had to think about if all he was going to say was no.

"I already talked to Wynn. Are you sure there wasn't anyone else?"

"Not that I saw."

That came out with no hesitation.

"What about someone you didn't see? Do you have a reason to think someone was there?"

"Had to be, didn't there? To poison Mr. Sawyer's coffee?"

"Yeah, there did. Do you have any idea who?"

"No."

Flat. No. No Connie Marina. Andrew was either the only

person at the lake who hadn't heard the rumors or the first one who didn't want to repeat them. Or maybe the first who knew a different set. Except for Wynn Everett, I still wasn't sure what he thought.

"You chauffeur Vince a lot, don't you, when he's here at the lake?"

"At least two weeks a year, sometimes more. For fifteen years now."

"Can you think of anybody who might want to kill him?"

"No."

The limo gleamed. Andrew stood back to admire his work.

"Not even his wife?"

"I've never believed the stories about her."

"What about other women?"

"Mr. Marina occasionally entertains in this house. As far as I am aware, all of his guests have been on good terms with him." He turned and looked at me. "I really don't know anything that would help you, Miss O'Neal. I'd tell you if I did."

"Sure. Thanks. And thanks again for polishing my car."

"You're welcome."

He walked away, around the side of the house, without looking back.

Vince was in his spot, glass in one hand and cigarette in the other, when I entered the living room. He nodded to me as if he had no memory of the night before. Probably he didn't. That's one of the few advantages of being a drunk—you can forget everything embarrassing at best, disclaim responsibility at worst.

"I talked to Connie," I said. The coffee urn was still out on the sideboard, and I poured myself a cup. It had been sitting on warm for a little too long, but I've drunk worse. I make worse.

Vince waited for me to go on.

"She admitted she's tried to kill you—said to tell you that sooner or later she'd do it, but I think that was mostly swagger. She says she had nothing to do with the barbiturates in Sawyer's coffee. And I believe her.''

I paused, hoping Vince would leap in with a comment, but he didn't.

''Vince, I think somebody else tried to kill you, somebody who knew Connie would get blamed for it. Do you have any ideas?''

He shook his head.

''I'm a nice guy,'' he said, turning to me and smiling, as if it were a joke between the two of us. ''No enemies.''

''Try to think of somebody who disagrees with that.''

He shook his head again. Back to the window. Drunks have an almost unlimited capacity to deny reality.

''Vince, listen to me. I believe your life really is in danger, and it isn't from Connie. Everybody around you is in danger, too, because the other would-be killer doesn't care who gets in the way. And I can't be your bodyguard and dig into who that person might be at the same time. You need somebody with you every minute, somebody who does everything but stand next to you when you pee, and even that wouldn't be a bad idea.''

He thought about that. I waited him out.

''Okay. Stay tonight. I'll tell Benny to have someone else here tomorrow morning.''

''Leaving me still in your employ, and free to ask questions?''

''Sure, honey. Do what you want to do.''

I had an impulse to quit, that was what I wanted to do. Let the bastard get killed. Except that I had accepted the job, and I had a responsibility. And I had been on the plane that almost crashed, and so had Sandra, and somebody else innocent might be with him the next time. Besides, I needed the money.

I absolutely did not want to sit there in silence until dinnertime watching Vince destroy his lungs, his liver, and the rest of his internal organs as well. There had to be a book or a magazine somewhere in the house. I looked around the living room/dining room and didn't see anything, though,

and I didn't want to ask Vince. Nothing in the halls, either.
I worked my way to the kitchen.

"Masaka, is there anything to read in this house?"

He jumped, startled at my sudden entrance or my
question or something. He was stuffing two chickens with
something fragrant. I was glad I was staying for dinner.

"Yes, miss," he said. "Under the stairs."

He turned back to his chicken.

There was a door to a small storage area under the stairs,
and inside was a collection of books that looked as if it had
been bought by the pound from a used-book store, topped
by some worn paperbacks that had doubtless been left
behind by guests that read. Or sort of, anyway. The stuff
was heavy on male fantasy trips. I pushed them aside and
picked up a dusty copy of *The Scarlet Letter*. I had read it
in college, so I knew how it ended, in case I had to leave it
behind, and it wouldn't hurt me to look at it again. I carried
it back to the living room, just to be close to Vince, and
settled on the couch.

That's how we were when Benny arrived. Vince had
moved twice to refill his glass and light a new cigarette. I
had turned pages.

"Hey, guys, what's going on?" Benny asked, when I
would have thought the answer obvious.

"Benny, make a couple of calls and get a new bodyguard
up here first thing in the morning," Vince said.

"Why? I thought we were all doing swell."

Benny looked at me, distressed, and I started to like him.

"We are."

I told him about my conversation with Connie and what
Vince and I had decided. He brightened up.

"That's a great idea. Vince, that's definitely the right
decision."

Benny chattered on until dinner, stopping only once,
when Tommy Durant arrived. Benny must have felt talking
was part of his job. I would have preferred Hawthorne's
company, but I felt compelled to nod at the right time.

The roast chicken was worth staying for. After dinner,

Vince took a short nap and I read until we all piled in the limo for the trip to the Seraglio.

I figured nothing was going to happen while Vince was on stage—the Seraglio had its own security, and I made sure they were aware of the problem—so I sat in a corner of Vince's dressing room and prepared to spend the evening with the adventures of Hester, Arthur, and Roger.

Until I heard voices in the hall. I had almost forgotten about Demetria Jones.

I opened the door.

"It's okay, Benny," I said. "She's with me."

"Yeah, but Freddie, I don't think Vince wants to see her."

"Sure he does."

Benny wavered, and Demetria slipped past him.

"Thanks," she said as I shut the door.

"No problem."

"Does he really want to see me?"

I thought about that.

"No."

She sat down in the chair in front of Vince's dressing table and put her head in her hands. She looked like a sad child, and I realized she wasn't much more than that. Vince's daughters were probably older than she was. She lifted her head and caught my eyes in the mirror.

"What did he say? What did Vince say when you told him I wanted to see him?"

"I told him you wanted to make sure he was all right. He asked me to tell you that he was."

Her head dropped again.

"But I'm not his messenger," I added, "and if you want to stay until he gets back, it's fine with me. I won't let them throw you out."

"I don't think I'll stay." She took a long time to say it. "There doesn't seem much point."

She took even longer getting up. She turned and held out her hand. I offered mine as well.

"Thanks for trying," she said. Her shoulders were square and her voice was steady and her black eyes met mine.

Demetria Jones was one of the most beautiful women I had ever seen.

I stayed in my corner through the crowd between shows, the second show, and the crowd after the show. I sulked in the corner of the limo on the ride back to the house, and once there, I headed straight for my room. I had nothing to say to Vince. I read until I was ready to fall asleep, and I braced a chair under the doorknob when I turned out the light. I wasn't going to sleep with Vince, no matter what danger he was in, and I figured that if anything happened, the noise would wake me up.

It did. Sometime the next morning. The sun was streaming through the window, and someone was pounding on my door, rattling the doorknob, trying to dislodge the chair.

"Hang on!" I shouted, scrambling for my bathrobe.

I moved the chair and opened the door. The man who stood there was the bodyguard of your nightmares. Six-foot-six with demented eyes and a face rearranged by a steel fist. Biceps the size of a giant sequoia, partly covered by a white T-shirt that could sail a yacht.

"You bitch!" he roared, grabbing the doorposts. "You whore!"

I froze, too terrified even to slam the door on his fingers. Anyway, I would have bet on the fingers.

"What the fuck kind of a bodyguard are you? How can you dishonor a noble profession like this?"

I couldn't come up with an answer, but he didn't wait long anyway.

"I get here this morning, ready to start work, and where's my client? Dead on the beach!"

Chapter 4

SOMEONE WAS POUNDING on my door. I figured it was a nightmare, and I wasn't going to get up and open the door just to hear all over again that Vince Marina had been murdered. So I tried to persuade myself to sleep through it. But the pounding persisted, and then I heard a voice, too. The voice was new, not part of the nightmare.

"Freddie! I know you're there! Open the goddamn door, Freddie!"

I opened my eyes to discover my own bedroom, with my own strewn clothes, and my own nylon curtains that were dusty black at the top and various shades of beige the rest of the way down. The sun shone brightly through a crack in the blind, casting a lightning bolt across my faded, flowered quilt. I really needed to do something about this. I should strip the bed and the windows and pick up everything and go to the Laundromat. Just as soon as I took care of whoever was pounding on my front door.

"I'm coming!" I yelled, putting on my bathrobe.

The pounding stopped.

The front door had been unlocked. Only the chain was holding it. I peeked through the opening and saw Deke standing there, his face an ugly dark maroon.

"I almost kicked it in," he said. "That chain couldn't hold back shit."

"Yeah, okay. Come on in."

I unhooked the chain and padded to the bathroom. I didn't

need to go as much as I needed to be alone for a minute, to gather my wits before I talked. I brushed my teeth and my hair and threw some water in my face.

"Do you want coffee?" I called, thinking the kitchen would be one more distraction.

"Not that pig swill you fix," he yelled back.

I gave it up and returned to my office. He had moved his bulk over the threshold, but that was about it. He loomed in the doorway like a thunderhead.

"I guess I should have called you," I began.

"Is that what you guess? I hear on the radio, on my way to work last night, that Vince Marina was found dead yesterday morning. I don't have any way to get in touch with you, find out what's going on. I come over this morning to check on your cats, just in case those two wild Indians you call pets managed to eat everything I left for them yesterday. And here's your car in the driveway and your chain on the door. And you guess you should have called?"

"All right. I'm sorry. I should have called. Thank you for looking after the cats and thank you for being concerned. Now, do you want to sit down?"

"If you can spare the time."

"Cut it out, please. I've had a tough couple of days."

We looked at each other, and the color in his face got a little better.

"Listen, you're right," I said, as brightly as I could. "I make lousy coffee, and I would really like a cup of something better. Hang on while I throw some clothes on, and let's go over to the Mother Lode."

"Okay, but hurry it up. I haven't eaten since I got off work, and I'm hungry."

I went back to the bedroom and looked for something clean to put on. Or something not too grungy, anyway.

I found an old pair of jeans with a torn knee and put them on. On Cher they would have been sexy, but they just made me look like a street kid, which was okay, since that was about how I felt. I added an even older UNR sweatshirt and went back to the office.

"Shit," Deke said. "You look like an overgrown twelve-year-old wearing hand-me-downs."

"Don't start on me," I warned. "We're going out for breakfast, not the Governor's Inaugural Ball."

"I just don't understand why you never want to look pretty. You looked good that one time you got your hair done, and a little makeup never hurt nobody."

"Then you wear it."

We glared at each other and left.

Virginia Street in the daytime looks cramped and old, too narrow for the cars and the people and the pale, flashing lights. I sometimes wish the casinos would turn off the neon, because it looks honky-tonk and embarrassing with the sun shining on it. It's the same feeling as watching the machinery work at Disneyland. Once you get inside, though, the daylight is gone, and the glitter and the hustle are the same at nine in the morning as they are twelve hours later.

As we threaded our way to the Mother Lode coffee shop, I told Deke the story, up through Arnie Lagatutta, Vince's never-to-be bodyguard, grabbing me by the arm and dragging me down to the beach to see the corpse.

We sat at a booth, and Deke slapped my hand as I reached for a Keno ticket.

"So then what?" he asked.

"So then nothing," I said, rubbing my hand. "Vince was lying there, sprawled on the sand, as if he had fallen off the porch. In his dressing gown. With an overturned glass, just out of reach. I looked at him, and Arnie Lagatutta yelled about what a fuck-up I am, and then after a while he let go of my arm, so I went back in the house to get dressed before the state police got there. Arnie had called them before he woke the rest of us up."

"Hi, Deke," said a fiftyish waitress with a pot of coffee in her hand. The uniform looked like a hand-me-up, as if it belonged to her daughter, with its puffed sleeves and above-the-knee skirt. Her teased hair and harlequin glasses were fifties' retro. "Coffee?"

"Yeah, for two," Deke said. "And I'll have ham and eggs, over easy, with biscuits."

"Bacon and scrambled. Yeah, biscuits," I added. They sounded better than toast.

"Orange juice?"

We both shrugged, and the woman nodded and left.

"What'd the police say?"

"Nothing. They took statements from Benny, Masaka, Andrew, Arnie, and me, took pictures, zipped Vince into a body bag, and then most of them left with the ambulance. Two guys strung a lot of yellow tape around the house and sort of wandered around watching while we packed our stuff and left. Benny, Masaka, and Andrew took the limo to the Seraglio. Arnie drove off in his Land Rover in the same direction. I came home."

"Feeling real proud of yourself?"

"Fuck off. I feel like shit."

The waitress had taken our shrugs in the affirmative, and she placed a freshly poured glass of reconstituted orange juice in front of each of us. With a smile.

"Then why don't you go back and do something about it?"

"Like what?"

"Like at least find out what happened. Probably it wasn't something you could have stopped, even if you'd known it was coming."

I shook my head.

"I don't know, Deke. Probably you're right, I couldn't have stopped it. What I think happened—my best guess without seeing the autopsy report, which won't be available for another forty-eight hours—is that the same person who doped Dean Sawyer's coffee doped Vince's vodka, with the same barbiturates, and in this case they were fatal. If that's it, I couldn't have done anything, because this isn't the Middle Ages, and kings don't have tasters anymore, to make sure their food isn't poisoned. I couldn't test every substance Vince Marina ingested to make sure it was okay. And if I'm right, the police are in a better position than I am to find out who killed him. Just trace the barbiturates."

"You're dreaming, girl. Nobody traces barbiturates."

"Yeah, okay, whatever. Anyway, this isn't like you. Usually you'd be telling me to butt out."

He took a sip of his coffee.

"I know. But usually it isn't any of your business. This time you got hired to do a job, and you didn't do it."

I winced.

"All right, it wasn't your fault. But you ain't gonna know that for sure until you follow it to the end."

"I'll think about that," I told him. "I'll think about it after I find out what's in the coroner's report."

Two large plates appeared on the table, with meat and eggs and potatoes, garnished by parsley sprigs on a slice of withered orange. The smiling waitress moved our unfinished glasses of orange juice to make room for the two smaller biscuit plates and the butter plate and the jam dish. I wondered how four people could manage breakfast in the booth. I wondered how I could eat, with Vince Marina dead.

"So," Deke said. "Probably you ate a big dinner when you got home last night."

He split a biscuit, opened a pat of butter, and spread it over a half. I watched the butter melt. He dipped one side of the biscuit half in his egg yoke and took a big bite.

"Was it Friskies or Nine Lives?" he asked.

"I don't remember," I told him, picking up my fork. I could eat pretty well, even with Vince Marina dead.

Deke and I went our separate ways after breakfast. The food had made me feel a little better. What Deke said had made me feel a little worse.

I walked down Virginia Street with my head down, threading my way among tourists who should have been enjoying the mild June morning but who were instead intent upon finding the perfect game of chance on which to drop the last of their discretionary dollars, and even some of their nondiscretionary ones, the ones that should have been marked for rent or food or bus tickets home. I was scowling, trying to think of something I could do without waiting for the autopsy report, when I almost bumped into a large, white T-shirt that blocked my path.

"Hey, Freddie, great to see you," rumbled over my head. I looked up at Arnie Lagatutta.

"I was going to call you—Benny Elcano gave me your number. You want to get a cup of coffee?"

His eyes had lost the demented glare, but his face didn't look any handsomer, even with an expression that was probably supposed to be a smile on it. And my arm throbbed where he had grabbed me the day before.

"No. I don't want coffee."

"Well, then I'll walk with you wherever you're going, and we can talk on the way."

I was going home, and I really didn't want him coming with me. On the other hand, he was too big to lose in a dark alley. We were only a couple of blocks from the small open green space—I can't call it a park—in front of the library, and I decided that if he hadn't finished talking by the time we reached it, I would sit on a bench until he got tired and left.

"Okay," I said. "Come on."

"I wanted to apologize for my behavior yesterday," he said, falling into step beside me.

I stopped dead and turned.

"You what?"

If I had listed all the things he might have said to me, an apology wouldn't have been one of them.

"I want to apologize."

Even clear, his eyes made me nervous. I started walking again.

"I was out of line yesterday. I shot off my mouth without knowing the whole story. After you left, Benny told me the rest of it, about the ex-wife and everything, and how Vince hadn't really wanted a bodyguard. There isn't too much you can do if the client won't cooperate."

"Thanks. Thanks a lot."

"You're welcome. It just upset me, you know, finding my client dead like that."

"Yeah, sure. It would have upset me, too."

What the hell was I doing comforting this guy?

"I guess the cops will pick up the ex-wife in a day or two, and that'll be the end of it."

"Right. Connie Marina is the obvious choice."

I was uncomfortable with that, but there didn't seem to be any point in telling him so.

We walked in silence until we reached the park.

"Anything else?" I asked.

Arnie was wearing a dark blue windbreaker over his T-shirt, and he hunched his shoulders in it, like a little kid. A young kid. Arnie wasn't little.

"I'm gonna be in town for a few days," he said, not looking at me. "I thought maybe we could have dinner one night."

I stared, panic-stricken, at the side of his face.

"No," I said. "No, I don't think so. I'm busy for the next few nights. For a while, really. Listen, I turn here, so I'll see you some other time."

I strode purposefully through the park, and he didn't try to follow. I kept going until I reached Mill Street, where I stopped until my heart rate calmed down.

Once I got home, I couldn't figure out what to do next. I turned on the computer and picked Adventure.

Two days later I was arguing loudly and vehemently— and I thought convincingly—with the state police sergeant who had taken my statement, insisting that under the circumstances I should receive a copy of the autopsy, when my doorbell rang. The sergeant didn't share my conviction.

"Just a minute!" I shouted, slamming down the phone.

I would have to call Sandra, who would doubtless be able to get it for me, or at least find out what was in it. Actually, I would have to return her calls. She had left three messages on my machine, and I hadn't returned them because I hadn't wanted to talk about Vince.

I threw open the door to find David Troy standing on my porch. A pale, sober David Troy, dressed for a yachting party in a navy-blue blazer, light slacks, and an open-necked white shirt. No ascot.

"I need to talk to you," he said.

I invited him in and pointed toward one of the folding chairs in front of the desk.

He looked vaguely around the room and sat. As he passed me I could smell that antiseptic odor that dry alkies give off. There were a couple of nicks along his jawbone where he hadn't shaved quite right.

"The police arrested Connie."

I nodded and sat down behind my desk. I hadn't heard, but I had expected it.

"The autopsy report said Vince died from a combination of barbiturates and alcohol."

I nodded again.

"Connie has a prescription for that same barbiturate. It seems the police checked, in advance. They were just waiting for the report to confirm the cause of death before they picked her up."

I couldn't pretend surprise.

"I want to hire you to help her."

That surprised me.

"After the great job I did protecting Vince?"

"I don't know who else to ask."

He said it simply. Flatly. Looking dazed, as if someone had hit him a little too hard, but he hadn't fallen over yet.

"I'm sure Connie has an attorney, and that attorney will recommend a private eye if he"—I used the word advisedly—"thinks it necessary."

"I suppose. But the difference is that you think she might be innocent. I can't count on her attorney believing her. Connie can be difficult, and she was rather outspoken about her efforts to harm Vince. Her attorney may jump to the same conclusions the police did. Roland Wence has agreed to take the case, by the way. He's flying up from L.A. this afternoon to arrange bail. Not that he won't try to get her off—I'm sure he'll do the proper lawyer things, like picking a sympathetic jury and looking for technicalities. But he may not believe she didn't do it, and he certainly won't bother to look for who did. That's what I want you to do—find out who did it."

I was surprised again. I didn't think much of my

conversation with Connie had penetrated his morning buzz.
And I was curious about who was putting up the money to
pay Wence. His retainer had to be five figures, and I
wouldn't be surprised if it was six. Maybe Connie was
mentioned in Vince's will. I'd have to find out who else was
mentioned.

"You're right. I don't think she did it. And whether
Wence believes her or not, his style is courtroom theatrics,
not working with an investigator. Okay, I'll do it, but I need
money up front, and I can't promise results."

"I understand that."

Troy took his checkbook and a silver pen from the inside
pocket of his blazer and looked for a clear spot on the desk.
I moved some papers aside.

"How much?" he asked. "I want it to be enough so that
you'll set everything else aside while you work on this."

"No problem," I said. "I charge five hundred a day, plus
expenses, and I'd like a week in advance."

I'd learned my lesson with Vince. I hadn't seen my two
days' pay, and I wasn't likely to under the circumstances.
Troy wrote the check without blinking, tore it out, and
handed it to me.

I took the check with as much nonchalance as I could
muster. I had seen checks for more, but none that I had
actually cashed.

"Thanks. Did you write the check for Wence, too?"

"Yes. And I'm sure you're wondering why. I'm doing
this because I love Connie."

My expression must have given away the fact that I
hadn't found her exactly lovable.

"She's not like that all the time," Troy added hurriedly.
"She could be unpleasant when she was talking about
Vince, true, and fantasizing his murder was something of an
idée fixe, but she was doing that less every day, and the rest
of the time she was warm, thoughtful, charming. . . ." He
trailed off, then continued. "I'm saying *was*. I suppose
that's a measure of how frightened I am."

"Frightened?"

"Yes. Frightened that she'll be taken away from me, for

one thing. Frightened that whoever killed Vince won't stop there, for another. I've never known anyone who was murdered before. And it's made me feel vulnerable.''

He looked vulnerable, and I felt sorry for him.

"Connie trying to kill Vince didn't make you feel vulnerable?''

"No, of course not. She was explosive, and certainly when Vince was right there in front of her she did try to kill him, but she wasn't capable of plotting his murder. And her ill will toward him was built over years of poor treatment and neglect. I thought that as long as I could just keep her away from him—I thought that time would heal her.''

"How did she handle the news of his death?''

"She was stunned. Benny Elcano called and told me, and I broke the news. I knew she was the obvious suspect, and I urged her to leave the country. We could have been in Spain before they issued a warrant.''

"Why Spain?''

"Friends of mine own a place in the country near Seville. Tracing us there would have been difficult.''

"So why didn't she want to go?''

Troy shook his head. He replaced the checkbook and pen in his pocket, preparing to leave.

"I don't know. She seemed to think her innocence would protect her. I tried to explain that the American judicial system isn't about guilt and innocence, only about verdicts. She was too upset to listen. Guilt and innocence aside, leaving would have been simpler than all this.''

"And less expensive.''

He smiled briefly.

"That, too.''

He stood up, so I did. He didn't hold out his hand.

"One more question,'' I said. "I thought you were staying with Connie, at the lake. Why can't you provide an alibi?''

"We sleep in separate bedrooms. And I'm afraid I sleep rather soundly. I couldn't swear that she didn't leave and come back in the night. Or, I suppose, any other time.''

A definite disadvantage of drunken stupors. They destroy

alibis. He made an attempt at a smile. All it did was twist his mouth.

"We must stay in touch, Miss O'Neal."

"Yeah, sure. Let me know when Connie gets out of jail."

He nodded and left.

I sat there at my desk and stared at the check. I had an awful feeling I was going to earn the money.

Chapter 5

I THOUGHT ABOUT Connie Marina on my way to the lake—the fast way, down 395 to Carson and up 50 to South Shore. No more dawdling in the pines. I was facing the prospect of too many trips for that. I thought about Connie Marina's anger, and why I didn't believe she had killed Vince.

My mother came home with a new perm one afternoon and discovered that in the two hours she had been gone, my father had cleaned out his half of the closet. He hadn't left a note, although about a week later he sent her a postcard confirming that he wasn't coming back. When I got home from high school, she was sitting in the living room, half a bottle of bourbon into the wind. She sat there for days, silent and drunk, until the postcard arrived. Then she exploded. Screamed, cried, tore the postcard to pieces, and burned the pieces. She never did tell me what he had said.

She looked around for something else to destroy, anything he'd left behind. She tore up books that he'd read, emptied the medicine chest because he'd touched the toothpaste. That was when I hid his jazz collection in my room. I knew if she thought of the records, they'd be gone. And at the time, I hoped maybe I'd see him again, and he'd be glad I kept his records.

My mother broke glasses, smashed dishes. Finally, she went to bed. She must have gone to the bathroom from time to time during the next several days, but never when I was

around. I would get up in the morning, get myself ready, go
to school, come home, and go to my room. Whatever I ate,
I fixed. We didn't see each other. We were living alone in
the same house.

One day she got up, took a shower, and cleaned up the
mess. And that was the end of it. Except that for a while she
would have eruptions of grief at awkward moments, like in
restaurants and movies, where she would suddenly start to
cry, and just as suddenly stop. She knew she had to either
get a job or find somebody else to marry her, and marriage
seemed the better choice, so she started calling all her old
friends.

Everybody who grew up in Reno has old friends. The
Reno High and UNR reunion committees have an easy job
of it, because so many graduates never get around to
leaving. In my mother's case, some of them were from a
pretty good social class, better certainly than my father's.
Those were the ones she started to see. She lived on credit
cards until she got married again six months after he left.
My stepfather cheerfully paid her debts—including the
lawyer's bill for the divorce.

I think my mother might have wanted to kill my father—I
would bet that she thought about it, even. And if she had
seen him, she might have tried. Another woman would have
thought of killing herself, not him, but my mother was a
survivor, and her anger never turned inward. She wasn't the
problem—he was. And she knew it. But with all her anger,
all her fury, she never tried to track him down, never plotted
revenge.

In a way I couldn't quite define—aside from the obvious
similarities in the situation—Connie Marina reminded me
of my mother. The difference was that Vince hadn't
disappeared, so Connie was always reminded that she
couldn't have what she wanted from him. I think my mother
would have restarted her life anyway, not become obsessed
the way Connie Marina had, but who knows. I wondered if
my mother would understand how lucky she was. Someday
I would have to tell her.

As I downshifted for the left turn at the junction with

Highway 28, which would take me to Zephyr Cove and Stateline, I shifted mental gears as well, to form some kind of plan. First stop would be the guest house, to see if Andrew and Masaka were still there. Or anyone else. Then, the Sultan's Seraglio. Somebody had doped not only Vince's vodka, but Dean's coffee as well. The Seraglio was the place to start looking for answers to that one.

I turned into the gravel driveway of the Seraglio guest house about two in the afternoon, late enough that anyone staying there would be up and about. No cars were in the driveway, and the house looked empty. I parked and knocked just to make sure, but the house had that hollow look houses get when something weird happens and everyone leaves. When no one answered the door, I walked around to the beach.

The day was crisp and breezy, and I was glad I was wearing a denim jacket. There were a few boats dotting the lake, white sails shining in the bright mountain sun, but the people in them must have been nuts. Or at least cold and wet.

I couldn't find the spot where Vince Marina's body had been. I'm not sure why I wanted to, what I thought I could find there, but I searched for some sign of his mortality. The yellow tape was gone, and the beach was clean, soft, pearl-gray sand. I looked up at the porch, the chair where I sat eating breakfast, the sliding glass doors to the house. The afternoon sun had turned the glass to a single white shimmer, so I couldn't see the spot where Vince had always stood with his drink and his cigarette, looking out.

There didn't seem to be much point in staying. I got back in the Mustang and drove the three miles to the hotel.

The Seraglio parking lot was filled with California license plates, savvy tourists catching the last couple of days before June 10, when the summer rates kicked in, so I had to drive to the third floor to find a spot. I took the pedestrian bridge straight to the casino, on the second floor of the hotel.

I was working my way through the red haze to the bank of elevators that would take me to the executive offices when I spotted Tommy Durant at a craps table. I stopped to watch. I wanted to talk to him, but this clearly wasn't the moment. White stubble showed on his cheeks, and his sweatshirt showed rings of dried sweat in the armpits. He picked up the dice with the hollow-eyed intensity of an addict cruising along on high. His point was eight, and he bet the hard way and made it. Then he picked up the dice again. I left. Sooner or later he was going to crap out, and I didn't particularly want to see him come down. Since he was evidently still staying at the hotel, I could catch him another time.

The Seraglio executive offices were up one floor, but they belonged to a different world. My boots sank into the pile of the pale blue carpeting. The pale blue walls were those of a museum gallery, one dominated by a large Renoir of a woman with a parasol, another by a Cézanne landscape.

"Personnel is downstairs, between the casino and the convention area."

The receptionist had sized me up and made her judgment while I was staring at the Cézanne. She had that California-girl look, hair permed to a crinkle, bleached four different shades of blond, and sprayed to look as if she had just grabbed hold of a high-voltage line. Her leopard-print blouse was cut low enough to show off a tan probably gained through daily lunch hours at the Seraglio's glass-enclosed pool. Not eating. Women that thin don't spend their lunch hours eating.

I handed her my card.

"I'm looking for a couple of Seraglio employees," I told her. "I need to talk to someone who has the authority to give me some information."

She looked at the card as if she had never learned to read and shifted uncomfortably in her chair.

"What is this in regard to?" she asked.

"Vince Marina."

"I heard they picked up his ex-wife."

I stared straight into her vacant brown eyes.

"You aren't paid to make decisions. I want to talk to someone who is."

She picked up the phone and hit a digit.

"Mr. Battaglia, there's a private investigator here who wants to talk to you about Vince Marina." She listened and put down the receiver. "Through the glass doors, down the hall to your right, last office on the left."

The hall was a continuation of the Impressionist gallery. Anybody who wanted to know where the casino profits were invested had only to take a tour. The last door on the left was open.

I walked into a corner office with a view of the lake that would have left me unable to work. I would have spent my days either staring out the window or avoiding the office, needing to be part of the scene just out of reach.

The walls and carpet were the same pale blue as the rest of the floor. The only decoration was a subdued Monet haystack that almost lost out to the view of the lake, but not quite. A fortyish man wearing a tailored white shirt and yellow paisley tie was standing behind a large, kidney-shaped desk. His light brown hair was styled, and the discreet CB monogram on his shirt pocket meant it was expensive, but his face was round and he was just a little too bland and corporate to be attractive, no matter how hard he was trying.

"I'm Craig Battaglia," he said. "What can I do for you?"

The Battaglia family owned the Seraglio. The name of the casino had been chosen at least partly because it was a reminder of their own, the way Ernie Primm had picked Primadonna, figuring it sounded better than Ernie's or Primm's. Or maybe Pete Battaglia, Craig's father, didn't have quite the ego of Bill Harrah or Charlie Barrington, didn't feel quite as compelled to name his business after himself.

Pete Battaglia had been part of the post–World War II gambling boom, one of the founding fathers of the industry. I had seen him a few times, an old guy in a red flannel shirt who held up his jeans with miners' suspenders. His son had gone to Harvard Business School.

Craig Battaglia didn't hold out his hand and he didn't sit

down. I walked up to the desk and leaned on my knuckles. I was easily three inches taller than he, and I knew he wouldn't like looking up at me.

"Freddie O'Neal," I said. "I'm a private investigator, and I need to know where I can find a couple of your employees."

He gestured toward one of the two upholstered chairs at strategic distances from his desk, close enough to talk, far enough to preserve his space.

"Go on," he said, when we were both seated.

My chair was, of course, too low for my legs. He now became the taller, more imposing presence.

"A chauffeur named Andrew and a chef named Masaka," I told him.

"Something to do with Vince Marina? I heard they picked up his wife."

"They did, but not everyone thinks she's guilty."

He shrugged.

"Our employee addresses are confidential."

"Look, they'll be subpoenaed, you know that. It's just that I don't want to have to wait for a judge."

"This is, after all, Nevada."

He said it dryly, and under other circumstances I might have smiled. Nevadans are the intellectual descendants of the settlers who didn't make it across the mountains to California, and the miners who started back when they didn't strike it rich but were too worn-out to get very far; nobody will preserve the Old West values, uphold individual responsibility and the free enterprise system, unless Nevadans do. Especially if it means a posse and a hanging. Or, for a few of us, averting one.

"Right. And it seems to me you wouldn't want this dragged out any more than I do."

Battaglia thought for a moment, assessing how likely I was to stay in his office and argue with him.

"Masaka has been temporarily assigned to the executive dining room. I'll ask him if he'd like to talk with you. Andrew and his limo are back in the pool, in the basement of the parking garage. If he's not at the airport, you can find him there.''

"Thanks.''

He picked up the phone, hit two digits, and asked for Masaka. After a short conversation, he replaced the receiver.

"The executive dining room is on the northwest corner of the floor. Monica can direct you if you get lost. Masaka will meet you there.''

"Great. Just one more thing. I'd also like to talk with Stacy, the flight attendant on the *Odalisque*. Where could I find her?''

"She's what's known as a contingency worker—we call her when we need her. I'll have someone let her know you want to talk with her. You can check back with me on that one.''

"Thanks. Be seeing you, I'm sure.''

I dropped a card on his desk and left.

I walked the long corridor to the other end.

Masaka was waiting for me in a room that held half a dozen small tables, each covered with a pale blue cloth and dotted with a bud vase containing a single rose wreathed in baby's breath. He was wearing the same white jacket, the same moussed, spiky hair. The view from the windowed walls was a continuation of the one in Battaglia's office. For lunch, it made sense. No one works at lunch. As a break from the Impressionists, the long wall opposite the window had one of those huge, Dutch still lifes, with fruit and a dead rabbit on a table. Somebody had great taste.

"Hi,'' I said. "Thanks for seeing me.''

He nodded.

"I'm sure the police have already asked, and I hope you won't mind going over this again, but I need to know if anyone else was around, either that day or that night, who could have had access to Vince's vodka. There was you, Andrew, Vince, Benny, and me.''

"And the piano player, Tommy.''

"Of course, Tommy. He was there for dinner.'' I hoped

I could find him again, in better shape to talk. "Anyone else? Did you see Connie Marina?"

"No—but I did see Lisa."

"Lisa?"

"Lisa Marina. She was there."

"Vince's daughter?"

He nodded.

"When? Where?"

"I found her there about midnight. She said Vince wasn't expecting her, that she would wait for him."

"In the living room? In the dark?"

"Yes."

"Then what?"

"I don't know. I went to bed. She wasn't there in the morning."

"Did you tell the police?"

"Of course."

"Good. She may have been the last person to see Vince alive." But did she have a motive to kill him?

"Yes."

"What?"

He raised his eyebrows, and I realized he was simply agreeing with what I said, not answering my thoughts. But it left me a little flustered.

"Do you have any idea how long she stayed or where she went?"

"No."

"And nobody else."

"No."

"Okay, listen, I'm sure you have to get back to work." I started backing toward the door. "Thanks for your time."

He watched me leave, nodding.

I waved at Monica on my way back to the elevator, and quickly dropped down a floor to the red, smoky casino. Tommy Durant was no longer at the craps table. But he hadn't gone far. I found him a few feet away, on a bar stool, nursing a beer. He didn't look any better. I slid onto a stool next to him.

"Hey, Tommy, how ya doing?"

"Fuck off, asshole."

I thought about telling him that nobody who gambled money he doesn't have should call anyone else asshole, but restrained the impulse.

"I'm sorry. I guess you're still pretty upset about Vince, I can understand that."

Tommy looked at me, wild-eyed. As he moved I got a whiff of his body. He smelled as bad as his sweatshirt looked.

"We were together for almost forty years, longer than he was with his wife, and no, no, you can't understand that."

"Yeah, you're right. I can't understand that."

He eased a bit. That made him feel better, that I couldn't understand.

"She's been charged with the murder, you know."

He turned back to his beer.

"I didn't know," he said. "I haven't had the television on. But I'm not surprised. She threatened enough. She was sure to do it sooner or later."

"Not everybody thinks she did it."

"I don't know who else would have."

"I don't either."

We sat there in silence, me studying Tommy, Tommy studying his beer, for about thirty seconds. Then the bartender—a thin young man with a full head of dark hair and a runny nose—made it to our corner. Tommy drained his glass and held it out for a refill. I shook my head.

"It's just that Connie says she didn't dope Dean Sawyer's coffee, when the Learjet almost took all of us out," I said when the bartender left, "and I believe that. So I think there's somebody else around who wanted Vince dead. Maybe Connie killed him, maybe she didn't. But I'd like to know who else is involved."

The bartender slammed Tommy's new beer a little too sharply in front of him. Foam slopped over the top of the glass.

"I can't help you," Tommy said, grasping his new glass with both hands.

He didn't look as if he was going to change his mind. Not then, anyway.

"Okay. I'll see you later."

I took the pedestrian bridge back to the parking structure and searched out an elevator that dropped me to the basement. The limos were lined up, four gleaming gold chariots, with no sign of charioteers. Or anyone else. I took the elevator back to the third floor, found my Mustang, drove down the ramp, and turned right on Highway 50, back through the gauntlet of ugly motels and uglier fast-food joints, toward the airport.

One gleaming gold stretch limo was parked smack in front of the small main terminal. I considered parking smack behind it, but daring someone to tow you isn't a good idea if you aren't a stretch limo. I parked in the lot.

There was no sign of Andrew in the terminal. I was going to lean against the car and wait for him, blotting his perfect wax job, when I saw him coming out of Tahoe Aviation. He paused when he saw me, as if he wanted to duck back inside, but he realized it was too late.

"Hello, Miss O'Neal," he said politely. "Were you looking for me?"

"Yes. I wanted to ask you a couple of questions about the night Vince Marina bought it."

"I'm afraid I can't help you. I left right after all of you went inside, and when I came back the following afternoon, the police were there."

"You don't stay at the guest house?"

"No."

"Did you notice anyone around the house that night, other than Vince, Benny, Masaka, and me? Maybe Lisa Marina—or at least her car?"

"No. It was dark, of course, and I might not have noticed a car at the side of the house. But I didn't even see Masaka when I deposited the three of you."

"What about earlier, during the day—besides Tommy?"

"No. Just the people you've mentioned."

"If you think of anything—" I started, but he cut me off.

"I've told the police all I know. Now, if you'll excuse me—" That time he cut himself off.

I moved away from the car door. He nodded, got in, and drove away. Without a passenger. He could have been dropping someone off, of course. Or he could have been here chatting with Wynn Everett, the other person who hadn't tried to make a case against Connie Marina. I thought about talking to Everett again, but I wasn't sure what I could ask that he might answer, and I surely didn't want to see him for the fun of it.

My next stop was Connie Marina's house at the north end of the lake. There was a chance Wence had bailed her out and she was home, and she was my best bet for getting in touch with Lisa.

As I drove past the Ponderosa, I thought about the Cartwright brothers saddling up and riding their horses so casually to Virginia City, something that used to make me nuts whenever I saw the show. Forty miles of bad road should have taken them two days there and another two back.

The baby-blue Cadillac was in the driveway of the cedar house. Next to it sat a white Toyota with a rent-a-car sticker and next to that was a red Land Rover with a California plate.

David Troy answered the door, glass in hand. His sobriety had evaporated with the morning dew, and he had settled into a comfortable afternoon haze.

"Ah, good," he said. "I was hoping you'd show up while Roland was still here."

I followed him into the living room. Connie was sitting on the leather couch, wearing a dark green sueded silk suit, the kind of classy-but-subdued look people choose to make a good impression on the judge. She was staring dully at the toes of her shoes.

Wence was at the bar, squirting seltzer into something that had started out a rich, dark amber, like brandy. I had seen pictures of him, but he was more imposing in the flesh, Roman nose and square jaw and all. He was dressed like a Southern-California lawyer—tweed jacket, white shirt with dark tie, jeans, and cowboy boots. Reno lawyers mostly wear suits. Long gray hair curled around his shoulders, in defiance of the receding hairline that made an already high forehead into one from an Egghead cartoon.

Troy introduced us and offered me a drink. I accepted a beer. He was pouring the Bohemia into a frosted stein before I could tell him the bottle was okay.

Wence peered at me, focusing just over the tops of his wire-rimmed glasses, in a way that I was certain was meant to be unnerving. I held my ground and stared back.

"Well," he said, with a smile. If he couldn't unnerve me, he'd try charm. "And what do you have to report?"

I was even less likely to be charmed than unnerved. I waited until Troy had freshened his own drink and turned to join us, hoping to remind Wence that he wasn't the one paying me.

"Not much yet. Except that Lisa Marina was there the night Vince died."

"What?"

Connie stopped staring at her shoes and sat up.

"What do you mean Lisa was there?"

"Masaka, the chef, told me she was waiting for Vince when we got back from the second show. I'd like to talk with her."

"Lisa didn't kill him," Connie snapped. "She adored him."

"Okay. I'd still like to talk with her. And I'm sure Mr. Wence would, too."

Connie grabbed a cordless handset from the table next to the couch and punched out a set of numbers. We all waited while the phone rang.

"Lisa, this is your mother. I'm out of jail and at the lake and I want to hear from you."

She flicked the disconnect, dug an address book out of a large black handbag on the floor next to the sofa, flipped a couple of pages, and punched out another set of numbers.

"Hi, honey, it's Connie Marina. I'm trying to track down Lisa. Do you know where she is?" A pause. "Yeah, yeah. I'm doing fine. Thanks." A pause. "Yeah, thanks. Look, if you hear from her, tell her to call me at the lake." A pause. "Really? Thanks, kid."

Connie let the phone dangle from her hand.

"A girlfriend says she's here somewhere. She says Lisa drove up to the lake Friday."

"You haven't heard from her?" I asked.

"Not in months. Lisa and I are not on the best of terms."

"What about your other two children?"

"Chris is on location in New Zealand. He'll be here tomorrow. Ricky's in his room."

"Here?"

"Yeah."

"How long has he been here?"

"He flew up from L.A. Saturday morning. I called him—and Chris, too—right after the police arrived to tell me about Vince." Connie laughed dryly. "Ricky was sure I'd be arrested. He may even believe I did it."

"Then we'll have to talk with him, Connie." Wence had an easy, genial manner. Laid-back. "Remind him that the American judicial system is founded on the presumption of innocence, among other things, and from now on, he should keep any doubts he may have about your innocence to himself."

"You think I did it, don't you?"

"I think the prosecutors are going to try to prove you did, and my job is to provide you with the best defense money can buy. I don't know whether you did it or not. Since, however, I'm part of the system, I must presume your innocence."

Connie picked up a drink that had been sitting so long the ice was almost melted.

"You're an asshole, Roland. But David's buddies all say you're the smartest asshole around."

David was perched on the arm of the couch. He leaned over and patted her shoulder.

"Don't offend the man, Connie. He's here to help."

"Could I speak to Ricky for a moment?" I asked. "And could one of you give me a way to get hold of Benny Elcano?"

I was going to have to get out of there quickly, before I started disliking them too much to do the job.

"Ricky's room is at the head of the stairs, west wing. And if you have something to write on, I'll give you Benny's number."

I pulled a pad and pen out of my jacket pocket. Connie flipped more pages in the book and rattled off a phone number.

I thanked her and scribbled it down.

I edged my way out of the room and looked for the stairs. I took them two at a time to release a little nervous energy and knocked on the door at the top.

"Just a minute!"

Something with heavy claws was scratching at the other side of the door. When it opened, a man in sweatshirt and jeans, with a brown ponytail longer than mine cascading down his back, was holding the collar of a cheerful gray-and-white Siberian husky who playfully lunged for me. I jumped back so quickly I almost fell down the stairs. Fortunately, the man had a firm grip.

"Stay, King," he said. "I'm sorry—he still thinks he's a puppy."

"Some puppy. Is it a good idea for me to touch him?"

"Sure. He loves people."

I carefully held out a hand for King to sniff, then just as carefully scratched his ears. He wriggled in his master's grasp.

Ricky Marina had to be in his late twenties, but like King, he thought he was still a puppy. At least he looked like one, with his open, friendly face, like a sad, innocent version of his mother's. His eyes were red-rimmed, and he looked tired. He switched the collar from his right hand to his left and held the right one out as he introduced himself.

"Oh, right, the private eye," he said, when I told him who I was. "Come on in."

I followed him into a cedar-paneled room dominated by an old-fashioned four-poster and a massive chest of drawers topped by a large mirror. An open suitcase sat on a rack at the end of the bed. Other than curtains at the window, the room was undecorated. The guest room.

Ricky gestured for me to sit in the only chair, a comfortable recliner next to a reading lamp. He sat cross-legged on the bed, with King stretched out at his feet.

"I'm sorry if I'm disturbing you. But I'm glad I have a chance to talk with you, away from the others," I said.

"You're not really disturbing me. I'm up here because I didn't feel like being polite, and I don't drink. I'll join them later. I'll have to, for dinner. David's okay, but I can't stand that asshole Wence. David told me he'd hired you."

"Yeah. Listen—I'm sorry about your father, I really am. I still feel I should have done a better job protecting him."

"Dad didn't want protection. He said if she was going to get him, she'd get him. It wasn't your fault."

My guilt was instantly compounded by the fact that I had just put an obviously grieving son in the position of comforting me.

"I don't think she did it."

"Well, that's good. I'd hate to think you were taking David's money if you believed she was guilty."

We both managed to smile, but not quite freely.

"I have to ask this—do you know of anybody else who might have wanted to kill your father?"

"No, I don't. He was pretty easygoing, and I can't figure out why anybody would hate him that much. Except Mom."

"If you think she killed him, why are you here?"

"She needs me."

He said it flatly, simply.

"Were you close to your father?"

"Not really. We got along okay, and I think I could have gone to him if I'd ever been in bad trouble, and he would have paid my way out of it, but he wasn't the kind of father who coached your Little League team or anything. We just never spent that much time together. Now, of course, I'm sorry I didn't make more of an effort. I guess people always say that when it's too late."

"Yeah, I guess they do."

He dropped down to the floor and hugged his dog. The dog would have hugged back if he could.

"What about Lisa?" I asked.

"She was probably closer to him than anyone else. She'd stay with him sometimes, when he was playing here or Vegas. He'd buy her stuff, and he dazzled her the way he always dazzled women."

"Did you know she was there the night he died?"

"Really? No, I didn't know. I don't see Lisa much, and we haven't talked in a while. Where is she now?"

"I was hoping you'd know. Nobody else seems to."

He shook his head.

"Sorry. If you find out, and she wants to see me but doesn't want to see Mom, let me know. I'll meet her somewhere."

"If I see her, I'll tell her. Listen—nobody has said anything about any kind of memorial service for Vince. Wouldn't she show up for that?"

"Yeah, there's going to be one in L.A., but Mom has convinced everybody to hold off for a few days. She still thinks something will happen so she won't go to trial."

"I hope she's right."

"Me too."

He tried to smile again, but it didn't go any better this time.

"Well," I said, getting up. "Thanks."

"Good luck."

Ricky stayed on the floor with his dog, still trying to smile, as I left.

I said polite good-byes to the trio in the living room, promising to be in touch. It was a relief to be back in the Mustang, heading for home. The sun had already dropped below the mountains, and the June evening was chilly. I had liked Ricky. I was glad I liked somebody in the family. I hoped I could find Lisa soon, and that she would be as friendly.

Butch and Sundance were waiting for me on the front porch. I opened the front door, and by the time I had turned on lights and heat they were in the kitchen. Butch sniffed suspiciously at the hand that had touched King, but then was more interested in his dinner. There was nothing in the house for mine, as usual.

I checked my answering machine, intending to pick up messages and leave again. But the one from Sandra was insistent, and I had been putting her off long enough.

"Thank God you've finally called," she said. "Juanita Elcano Holt called me this afternoon. And Freddie, whatever you're doing, she says you've got to stop!"

Chapter 6

"ALL RIGHT, what's going on?"

I was waiting in a booth at Harrah's, halfway through a beer, watching the Keno board, when Sandra swept in. Sandra's husband, Don Echeverria, had some kind of meeting that evening, she hadn't eaten dinner, and we both felt the conversation was better held in person. And the Mother Lode was out because Deke would be there and want to join us and Diane would be hurt because we weren't sitting at her station.

"Let's order first, I'm starved."

The Keno board was starting to light up, without enough of my numbers, while Sandra glanced at the menu. I have to check carefully each time, because I always mark tickets randomly, so I never remember what numbers I've played. My idea of hell is walking into a casino and seeing the Keno board lit up with the eight numbers I always play. Except that I don't have a ticket in for that particular game.

The waitress took my order for fried chicken and another beer, Sandra's for broiled sea bass and a glass of white wine.

"Okay," I said. "I'm waiting."

"Well, really, I was hoping you could tell me. All I know is that Juanita called this afternoon to thank me for trying, but as long as Vince was dead and Connie charged, there was no point in your pursuing the matter. She specifically asked me to tell you that, and she sounded upset."

"Do you think Governor Reilly asked her to call?"

"Not necessarily. Since it was Benny who asked her to call me in the first place, he could have asked her to call you off, although I don't think that would have upset her. She wouldn't offer any information on who or why. All she said was that she had gotten me into this, and I had gotten you into it, and now I should get you out. Your turn."

I handed a dollar to the Keno runner, who nodded and left to place my ticket again. Sometimes I stayed with the same numbers for a couple of games, if I didn't want to fill out a new ticket. Sandra raised an eyebrow, but didn't say anything, the way she might if I lit a cigarette and blew smoke at her.

I told her the whole story, skimming over Vince's head in my lap, and mentioning Arnie's apology but not his dinner invitation. I was afraid she would think I should have accepted one of them. Either one.

"You really believe she didn't do it," Sandra said when I was through.

"Yeah, I do."

"Then you have to keep going, of course. And Benny becomes a suspect."

"I don't think so. I don't think Benny would have doped Sawyer's coffee. He didn't know I could land the plane. I didn't know I could land the plane."

"So Juanita didn't want you out to protect Benny. Do you think Governor Reilly is somehow involved?"

"Oh, hell, I don't know." The Keno board was lighting up again, still without my numbers. "Politics is your beat, not mine, and I don't know why the governor would want Vince dead and Connie blamed for it."

"I don't know why either, but if that's what it is, you have to find out."

"Thanks, Sandra. What would I do without you?"

She smiled sweetly. And the food arrived.

When the waitress had left, I asked, "What are you going to do about Juanita Elcano Holt?"

"Tell her how hard I tried. How stubborn you are. That sort of thing."

"Tell her I have a client and I need the money. That's the truth."

"What about you?" Sandra asked. "What do you do next?"

"Benny, I think. He's easier to reach than the governor. Besides, Juanita could have been doing a favor for any number of people when she called you and asked you for a favor. And she could have been upset about something else."

I was just picking up a chicken leg when a heavy hand fell on my shoulder. I turned and saw the looming torso of Arnie Lagatutta.

"Hey," he said. "Good to see you. I'm not meeting anybody. Can I join you?"

I shot a desperate look at Sandra, who missed it.

"Of course," she said, smiling at him.

We were sitting at a U-shaped booth, and she slid neatly into the middle, moving plate, place setting, and glass in a couple of smooth gestures. Arnie sat down opposite me, in Sandra's spot.

I introduced them, hoping both would catch my lack of enthusiasm. But Arnie held out his hand and Sandra shook it. They beamed at each other, like a couple of conspirators. Arnie held up a hand like a white flag and the waitress showed up immediately.

"A hamburger and a beer," he said.

"Right away."

I always like to sit on the edge of the booth, so my legs can go on the outside of the table. I try not to extend them into the path of innocent Keno runners and waitresses. So there was no room for Arnie's legs under the table. I hoped the waitress was trained in broken field running.

"So," Sandra said. "Freddie told me you're a professional bodyguard. How did you choose a career like that?"

I hoped she asked better questions when she was working.

"An accident," Arnie said, shaking his head and grinning, clearly pleased that we had been talking about him. "I was drafted right out of college by the Denver Broncos.

About halfway through my second season we were playing the Raiders in a heavy rain. I tackled the runner, the ball slipped out of his hands, I skidded sideways trying to get it, and three guys came down on my leg. No more football. Just down the hall in the hospital was a guy recovering from an assassination attempt. We met in the corridor one day while the nurses were exercising us. I stayed with him ten years. Since then, I've free-lanced."

"Who was he?" I didn't intend to be interested, but the question popped out.

"I'll tell you when I know you better," he said, still grinning.

Forget that.

"How did you end up working for Vince Marina?" Sandra asked.

I glared at her. That, of course, was the question I should have asked.

"A call from the Seraglio. I've done some work for them before, when they've had a headliner who feels vulnerable for some reason and they've wanted to beef up security."

"Where are you between jobs?" I asked.

"Southern California. The hills north of L.A."

"Then why are you still here?"

"The Seraglio asked me to stay. Why do you want to know?"

I bristled, and my face was probably flushed.

"Who calls you from the Seraglio?"

"A guy named d'Azevedo. Head of security. One more time, why do you want to know?"

He had a soft voice for such a big guy, and he sounded as if he was having a good time.

"Because you were the first person at the scene of a murder that the wrong person's been arrested for."

He nodded.

"Yeah, I heard you were hired by the ex-wife's new boyfriend."

"Who told you that?"

"Hey, listen, I'm on your side, I really am. Somebody

hired you to find out what you can, you're a professional with a job to do, I'll tell you what I know.''

"But?"

"But I don't think there's anything to find. I think this is one of those situations where the obvious answer is the right one.''

If there's anything I hate more than being grabbed by the arm and dragged out of my room, it's being patronized.

"So what do you know?"

I leaned forward onto the table.

"Nothing."

Arnie leaned forward, too. The strength of the Formica was tested, but it held.

"I got up there and Vince Marina was dead,'' he continued. "And everybody says it was his wife.''

His hamburger arrived just then, which was a good thing, because my chicken was getting cold. I hadn't stopped eating because I was polite. I just forgot for a minute.

"We have only your word that he was already dead,'' Sandra said blithely. She had almost finished her food. She motioned to the waitress that she wanted another glass of wine.

"Yeah, but he was,'' Arnie said, picking up his hamburger. "You can check out when I was called and when I arrived with d'Azevedo, at the Seraglio, against the time of death in the coroner's report.''

He took a bite and looked at me.

"Unless you think somebody at the Seraglio is involved,'' he added.

"I don't know yet.''

"Well, kid, some people like conspiracy theories,'' he said through a mouthful of burger. "But I always thought William of Ockham had the right idea—'entities are not to be multiplied beyond necessity.' When you have a simple solution—in this case one entity, the ex-wife—there's no reason to complicate it.''

"Ockham's razor, Philosophy 101,'' I snapped.

Arnie nodded, swallowed his mouthful.

"A useful concept,'' he said, "although not his own. It

was named after him only because of the extremes he carried it to.''

''And it sure as hell can't be used to prove Connie Marina murdered her ex-husband.''

''True.'' He washed the burger down with a gulp of beer. ''You might also quote Whitehead. 'Seek simplicity. Then distrust it.' But that's probably Philosophy 102.''

''I don't usually quote philosophers at all. I think it takes you in the wrong direction. We're not talking—I'm not talking—abstract principles here. Vince Marina has been murdered, by person or persons unknown, not his ex-wife Connie. I believe that. What I'm interested in is finding out who killed him. And sitting here talking about some damn theory isn't going to help.''

I reached for the check, but Arnie grabbed it.

''On me. I insist. And you're wrong. My late employer taught me that. A couple of evenings a week we would play chess and talk. Theories, concepts, and abstractions are the best way to deal with violent death. Otherwise, it is too terrible to bear.''

I had no answer, and I wanted to leave. I got up from the table, managing to avoid tripping over Arnie's legs.

''Thanks for dinner,'' I said.

Sandra scrambled after me. I could hear her saying the polite stuff about how pleased she was to have met him. She caught up with me as I was passing the cashier.

''Why were you so rude?'' she asked. ''He's obviously interested in you. And he's smart. You could at least have been nice to him.''

''I'm not interested in him. So don't play matchmaker.''

''I wouldn't dream of it. I just think that going out on an occasional date wouldn't be a fate worse than death.''

''Maybe not. But he makes me nervous. And he looks like Lurch.''

''Lurch?''

''From the old television series.''

''He does not.'' She laughed, though. ''He looks like what he is—an ex-football player who got hit in the face a couple of times.''

"More than a couple."

We rode down the escalator in silence.

"What are you going to do now?" Sandra asked.

"Try to get hold of Benny Elcano. Worst case, leave a message at the number Connie Marina gave me and hope he calls me back."

"You should have asked Arnie about him. Arnie might know if he's still around the lake."

"Yeah, I should have. Good night."

"Keep in touch. I hope you're right about Connie Marina."

Sandra turned toward the parking lot, and I started to thread my way through the roulette tables to the Center Street door. But the problem was, she was right. I should have asked Arnie if Benny Elcano was still around. I threaded my way back.

I got off the escalator just as Arnie was paying the cashier.

"Hey, great," he said. "You changed your mind."

"Not exactly. But I need to get in touch with Benny Elcano, and I thought you might know if he was staying at the lake. And catching you now seemed easier than calling you through the Seraglio."

He nodded.

"Good idea. I can put you in touch with Benny Elcano first thing in the morning. How about a movie?"

"What?"

"Well, your girlfriend is going home to her husband—I saw the ring—and you don't have any other plans. There's a female supercop movie at the Crest, and we'll be just in time for the eight o'clock showing. Wanta go?"

"To the Crest? Are you sure that's the one you want to see?"

"Yeah—I think women with guns are sexy. I thought you were sexy the first time I saw you, in your bathrobe, stunned and vulnerable, with your hair all loose and wild. But there's a lot of anger in you, and your anger is even sexier. Even without a gun."

I started to back away.

"Maybe this isn't such a good idea."

"No, come on. I understand anger, and I don't take it personally. I was angry while I played football, and angry in the hospital, angry in ways that I thought would never be right. It took years for me to work it out, talk it out. And I'm not going to mess with you. I like you. We're just going to a movie."

"There's a problem. We both need the aisle seat. I'm not sitting with my knees against my chest for two hours."

"First row of the balcony. We stick our feet through the rails."

"Okay. I pay my own way, though."

"Yeah, if you want. Let's go."

Walking with him was easy. I had almost noticed that the first time, but not quite. Our strides matched, and it didn't make him uncomfortable. I thought about breaking into a lope, or a canter, just to see if he would follow.

We were waiting for the light at the corner of Second and Virginia when I heard someone say, "Well, hello, Freddie. How are you? And who is your friend?"

Deke. Oh, shit. I had to introduce them. I could see how it looked to Deke—me standing there with Arnie, both of us in jeans and jackets, waiting for the light with our hands in our pockets. Like a date. And I just didn't feel like explaining.

Deke and Arnie shook hands firmly, the way guys do when they want to impress each other. No blood spurted from under their nails, but another ounce of pressure on either side and it would have. It was the first time I had ever seen Deke look short next to somebody.

"We gotta go," I said.

"Well, don't let me keep you," Deke said, with a fake smile on his face.

"Okay. I'll talk to you tomorrow."

"Fine. Of course. Whenever you have the time."

Arnie didn't ask who Deke was and I didn't volunteer.

The Crest is one of those old-fashioned movie theaters, the kind that hasn't been built in twenty years or so, not since the multiscreens in the minimalls became the law of

the land. At one time the Crest was Reno's most lavish film
palace, the plush seats and the gold drapes and the plaster
waves framing the proscenium all reminders of Gold Rush
opulence. The Crest had the first Cinemascope screen in
Reno, so it charged an extra fifty cents for admission,
flaunting its superiority to the other Reno houses, the
Majestic and the Granada.

The lesser two closed years ago, losing out to Cinemas
I–V and their equally nameless, unromantic, unadorned
cousins. But the Crest hung in, an aging dowager with
cracked skin and a molting fur stole, supported by Reno
moviegoers who remembered going to Saturday-morning
shows in the fifties where kids got in free with two tops
from Old Home milk cartons. The faithful drank their Old
Home milk and flocked weekly to see the new chapter in the
Superman serial and the latest from Roy Rogers and Dale
Evans. Years later, there was a new Superman, but nobody
ever replaced Roy and Dale.

I knew this because I worked as a cashier at the Crest
part-time one year while I was in college. I saw Indiana
Jones shoot the guy with the scimitar twenty-seven times,
because my break came at the same time every evening, and
it wasn't long enough to go anywhere or do anything except
watch a few minutes of the movie. I had to come in early
one Saturday to see the rest of it. I always liked the Crest.

Arnie let me pay my own admission, but he bought the
popcorn and the soda. One reminder that the Crest was not
what it used to be was the lack of an usher to tell us to put
our feet down. We stretched undisturbed. But then, it was a
weeknight, and the theater was two thirds empty. I hoped
we weren't watching the penultimate picture show.

After the movie, we started walking down Second.

"What'd you think?" Arnie asked.

"I think we're seeing the reemergence of the woman
warrior as an archetypal character in late-twentieth-century
American culture, but some of her appearances are in really
lousy movies."

He cracked up.

"That's great, that's just great. Come on, let's get a beer and talk about it."

"You really want to?"

"Yeah. One of the problems with being a bodyguard—or a football player—is that a lot of people think you must be dumb if that's how you make a living. I don't run across many people I can talk about ideas with."

I thought about that. I wasn't feeling quite as tense, after sitting next to him for two hours.

"Yeah, okay. I'll have a beer."

The Sierra Madre has a quiet bar, the Hideaway, that you can get to either from the street or the casino. We walked down Virginia a block and turned in there.

Talking to him got easier after the third beer. He really did like to talk about ideas, and didn't mind that I wouldn't let the conversation get personal. I didn't get nervous again until I got tired and realized I was going to have to end the evening somehow.

Arnie had started to signal the bartender for another beer, but I shook my head.

"Time for the check," I said.

"Okay. Where's your car?"

"I walked."

"Mine's in Harrah's garage. Walk back with me, and I'll give you a ride home."

"No point. It's just as close for me to walk home."

"Okay. I'll settle the check and walk you home."

He reached for his wallet.

"I'll split the check and I don't need anyone to walk me home," I said. "Reno is where I live, and I can take care of myself."

That came out a little tougher than I intended, but I got scared at the thought of Arnie coming home with me.

"Suit yourself." He leaned back in his chair and smiled. "But I need your phone number. I promised to have Benny Elcano call you in the morning, remember?"

"Benny has my phone number," I said. "And it's listed anyway."

"Okay. I had a good time tonight. I'd like to see you again."

I struggled with my wallet.

"Yeah, I guess so. I have a card. Here."

I tossed what I figured was my half of the bill on the table and my card on top.

"I'm staying at the Seraglio," he said, still smiling, "if you want to call me."

"Thanks, I'll remember."

My face was flushed, I could feel it, and as soon as I was out the door I paused for a moment to cool off before I started home. I was beginning to like Arnie, and I never know what to do when I'm beginning to like some guy. This is the kind of thing girls are supposed to learn how to handle when they're teenagers, but I spent my teens taller, smarter, and better coordinated than the guys my age, and nobody ever asked me out. Not one date did I have in high school. And nothing has happened since that has made relating sexually any easier.

I was so late getting home that Butch was curled up in the glow of my desk lamp—it's on a timer—and Sundance was asleep on the bed. Butch squeaked in mild outrage when I picked him up and carried him into the bedroom.

As I got ready for bed I thought a little about Arnie Lagatutta. And then about Vince Marina, and Benny Elcano, and how in hell was I going to find Lisa Marina if she didn't want to be found. But I'd had enough to drink that all of it left my head when I turned off the lights. It didn't even come back when a ringing phone woke me up and scattered the cats.

"I heard you were trying to get in touch with me," Benny Elcano said.

"Yeah, I need some information," I said. But I wasn't awake enough to remember what it was. "Is there someplace I can meet you?"

"Sure. I'm staying at the lake for a few days. How about the Seraglio coffee shop at noon?"

"See you then."

I struggled out of bed and into the shower. It was already ten o'clock, and I would have to hurry.

The Nevada Highway Patrol is pretty selective about enforcing the speed limit—it was federally imposed, after all, on a state that never had one before and doesn't like anything federally imposed anyway. And dark green Mustangs don't call a lot of attention to themselves at any speed. Still, I kept one eye on my rearview mirror as I raced along the flat stretch between Reno and Carson.

I made pretty good time up the four-lane section of Highway 50 and pulled into the Seraglio parking structure with a few minutes to spare.

Benny was waiting in a booth, this time wearing a strawberry sport shirt buttoned to his chin. He waved me over, and I sat down across from him.

"So you're working for Connie now," he said. He shook his head so sadly that his jowls flapped like a hound dog's.

"Why is that a problem?"

A waitress appeared bearing a massive tray. She placed an omelet with country fries and a separate plate with white toast and jelly on the table in front of Benny.

"Coffee?" she asked cheerfully.

"Yeah, thanks," I said. "And another of the same, what he's got."

She filled my cup and topped off Benny's. "Right away."

"I'm sorry," Benny said. "I wasn't sure when you'd get here. Do you mind if I start?"

"Not as long as you can talk and eat. What's wrong with my working for Connie—not that she is necessarily my client."

"Probably Troy is paying the bill. But whoever hired you, you're trying to prove she didn't do it. Why?"

Benny picked up a big hunk of omelet on his fork. Chicken livers. If I'd realized it was a chicken-liver omelet, I would have ordered something else. But it was too late to catch the waitress.

"Because I don't think she did it."

"She did it, Freddie, trust me, she did it."

"Proof, Benny. Did you see her around the house? Did anybody see her drop pills in Vince's vodka?"

He swallowed before he answered.

"No, but she was the one who tried before, I told you that. I saw her before."

"Yeah, but before he didn't die. This time, nobody saw Connie there, but somebody did see Lisa."

"Lisa? Lisa was there that night?"

"So I'm told. What do you know about it?"

He punctuated his answer with pounds on the bottom of the ketchup bottle as he held it over his potatoes.

"Nothing. She usually shows up while Vince is at the lake, and Vegas, too, but I hadn't seen her, and he hadn't told me when she was coming."

"Do you know where she usually stays when she's here?"

"With Vince, of course. At the guest house. There's lots of room."

"What about other women—I thought Vince sometimes had girlfriends at the guest house?"

"Yeah, but never while Lisa was around."

"Where would Lisa stay if she didn't stay with Vince?"

"I don't know. As far as I know, she didn't have any friends up here."

"Will you let me know if you see her or hear from her?"

Benny pondered the question while he spread grape jelly on his toast.

"I don't know. I may let her know what you're doing, see what she wants to do about it. But if Lisa doesn't want to talk to you, probably I wouldn't let you know."

"Thanks a lot."

My omelet arrived, and I wished I hadn't ordered it. I was going to have to talk to Benny longer than I wanted to if I planned on eating much of it.

"Listen, you gotta understand, I was with Vince a long time. I believe Connie did it, and I don't want her getting off on some technicality, because some smart lawyer has thrown a smoke screen in front of the jury. And there's no way you can make Lisa a suspect. Lisa adored Vince."

"Okay," I said, "I believe you. I'd still like to talk to her."

"Yeah, all right. Anything else you want to know?"

I nodded and swallowed.

"Did you see anybody else around the guest house that night or the next morning? Anybody unexpected?"

"Nobody you didn't see."

"Can you think of anybody other than Connie who might have wanted to kill Vince?"

"No. Absolutely not."

He looked me straight in the eye as he said it.

"Okay. Just one more thing. About your sister. Why did you ask her to get me off the case?"

"Juanita? I didn't ask her anything. I mentioned to her last week that Vince was looking for a bodyguard, but I didn't ask her anything about you. I didn't know you were connected to her, except through that reporter. And I didn't know you were asking questions about Vince until Arnie Lagatutta told me this morning."

"You didn't talk to Juanita yesterday?"

"Absolutely not, I swear it."

That wasn't the answer I wanted. The alternative could mean I was in deep water here.

"Tell me about Arnie Lagatutta," I said. "How'd you get involved with him?"

"Arnie? I've known him for years. He worked for the same guy for ten years—that's rare in his business."

"Who? Who did he work for?"

Benny shook his head, jowls flapping again.

"He can tell you if he wants to. I won't. Anyway, he does occasional security jobs for people, works for the Seraglio from time to time, that's it, as far as I know."

I didn't like the way Benny was studying me, so I concentrated on my food.

"He's never been married," Benny added.

"I didn't ask that."

"I know. But that was something I wanted to tell you."

"Yeah, okay."

I ate the potatoes and part of the omelet. I thought about

taking the rest of it to the cats, who like chicken livers, but I wasn't sure when I'd get home, and I didn't want them rotting in the car. I gulped some coffee.

"Where's the check?" I asked.

"Don't worry about it. I got a tab here."

I thought about arguing, then remembered I hadn't been paid for the two days with Vince.

"Okay. Thanks."

"And Freddie? I didn't ask my sister to get you off the case. But it might be a good idea. Connie has a good attorney. Let the courts handle it, all right?"

"Why? Why is it a good idea?"

Benny looked at me with sad hound-dog eyes.

"It just is. For whatever reason Juanita called—and I don't know what that was. But it means somebody wants you out of this. And I like you, honey. I don't want to see you in trouble."

"I'll remember that."

I was going to have to talk to Juanita. I said good-bye to Benny and left.

I was walking across the pedestrian bridge to the parking structure when a red-and-white paramedic ambulance went screaming underneath me, past the lobby entrance, and down the narrow road to the beach. Normally, I'm not an ambulance chaser. But I got goose bumps listening to this one. Maybe it was just the memory of Vince Marina's body. Anyway, I decided to see what was happening, who the siren howled for, before I left.

A crowd had massed around the ambulance in the time it took me to walk down the garage ramp and cover the few hundred yards from the hotel to the sand. But nobody in it was taller than Arnie's shoulder. I worked my way through to him.

"What's going on?" I asked.

"You don't want to see. They just pulled Tommy Durant out of the lake."

Chapter 7

I STOOD THERE, my way to the beach blocked by Arnie's bulk, not sure what to do. Benny's voice was in my head: "When his debts pile up, Vince talks to the Seraglio. Otherwise, Tommy'd be dead by now." No wonder Tommy was so upset when I saw him in the bar. He knew Vince wasn't the only dead man.

"How did it happen?" I asked.

"An accident. He had too much to drink, fell off the end of the pier, couldn't get out."

"Oh, Arnie. No way."

His eyes flickered, and he didn't try to stop me when I pushed past him.

I couldn't get as close as I wanted because two state cops were keeping people back. But I managed to get a glimpse of Tommy as he was loaded onto the stretcher. He was wearing the same sweatshirt and pants that I had seen him in the day before. One leg fell, dangled, as the stretcher was being lifted, and as the paramedic replaced it I noticed some kind of red mark around his ankle. His feet were bare—he probably lost his shoes in the water. I thought about that red mark, what might have caused it. I thought about how you could keep somebody in the water until he drowned. A weight tied to his ankles would do it.

I watched them slide the stretcher into the ambulance, close the doors. The engine started, and the crowd parted to let the ambulance through. No need for a siren now. I turned back toward Arnie. He wasn't alone. Craig Battaglia was on one side of him, and another ex–football kind of guy was on the other side. As I walked toward them Craig whispered something to a young woman with long, dark hair, who slipped away with the crowd.

"Freddie, you know Craig Battaglia, and this is Jack d'Azevedo, head of security," Arnie said.

I looked at both men. Nobody held a hand out.

"Any questions today, Miss O'Neal?" Battaglia asked.

"I'd like to hear about the last few hours of Tommy Durant, if nobody minds. I think the people who saw him in the casino are the ones to talk with."

"Jack's already done that."

Battaglia nodded toward d'Azevedo. I didn't point out how quick the inquiries had to have been.

"Durant was drinking most of the day. Bar in the corner of the second-floor casino, where you talked to him." D'Azevedo made sure I hadn't missed that. "He'd lost pretty heavily at the tables, and we cut off his credit. And I guess he was pretty despondent about the death of his old pal. So in the early evening he left the hotel, that's all we know. We figure he took a walk out to the end of the pier, fell in, and couldn't pull himself out. One of the paramedics checked his fingers—there were splinters where he tried to climb back up the pier."

"Who found him?"

"A guest from the hotel, out for an early-morning walk."

"Damn. If he'd only been able to float—he could have let the waves wash him to shore while he was still alive."

Battaglia and d'Azevedo stared at me. Arnie looked away.

"Who knows?" d'Azevedo said quietly.

"Sorry about the publicity," I said to Battaglia. "Two bodies on the beach, such a short time. It can't be good for the tourist trade."

Battaglia did something to his face that was supposed to be a smile.

"Just as long as the papers spell our name right, it's good for the tourist trade. A little tough on the guy who found the body—but we told him his room was on us, and all of a sudden he felt better about it. Decided to stay an extra couple of days, in fact.''

"Yeah, sure. It'll be a great story to tell when he gets home."

We looked at each other.

"Well," I added, "good or bad for the tourist trade, I hope this is the last body lying on the beach for a while."

"So do I, Miss O'Neal," he said politely.

"I gotta be going," I said.

Nobody said anything until I started off. Then Arnie called after me, "Hey, Freddie, I'll talk to you later, okay?"

I didn't look back.

I stopped in the hotel, found a pay phone in the lobby, and called Connie Marina's Tahoe number.

David Troy answered.

I told him about Tommy Durant—the official story, without the ankle mark.

"I didn't know Mr. Durant," he said. "Connie knew him, of course, and I'm sure she'll be saddened to hear he's dead. Could he have helped us—is this going to hurt our case?"

"I don't know. But I need to ask you something else. Describe Lisa Marina for me."

"Lisa? She's really very beautiful, in her midtwenties, long black hair. I might be able to find a picture, if that would help."

"Yeah, thanks."

I hung up. If the woman with Craig Battaglia had been Lisa Marina, he didn't want me asking her any questions. I could worry about that after I'd seen her picture.

My next stop was Carson City.

Juanita Elcano Holt's office was in the old capitol, erected in 1870, the earliest that the newly admitted state could raise the money. It's mostly a museum now—there's a new building for the legislature—but a lucky few still work in the stone-and-marble monument to the Victorian penchant for excess. I'm serious about the lucky. The new

building was designed when minimalism was the rage, and
it has no soul.

I walked the length of the bright mosaic listing all the
Nevada minerals, checked out the portraits of the Governors
of Nevada from Henry Goode Blasdel and L. R. "Broadhorns" Bradley to the present one, Timothy J. Reilly,
climbed the stairs, and finally found Juanita Elcano Holt's
officer in a corner of the second floor.

"Broadhorns" Bradley, by the way, is best remembered
not for his nickname—he got that for being an Elko cattle
rancher—but for the time the mine owners tried to bribe him
to veto a bill establishing a tax on gold and silver bullion by
sending him a blank check, telling him to write in any
amount he wanted. He tore the check up and signed the bill.
He lived, too. Of course, nobody ever asks what he would
have done if the tax had been on cattle.

Holt's door was open, and she was sitting behind her
desk. My first reaction was surprise that I didn't have to face
a phalanx of secretaries. But Juanita Elcano Holt wasn't
Governor Reilly's only assistant. She was the one known to
insiders, political reporters and fast-track people, not the
public. Normally, people didn't barge in on her. This wasn't
a normal time, and I didn't think making an appointment
would work anyway.

There was a family resemblance to Benny—the furrows
and the sagging cheeks that marked the beginning of jowls,
the sense that this person operated in a constant state of
anxiety. But she was softer, like a squirrel, not a hound dog.
I remembered we had thought Mrs. Elcano looked like a
squirrel when I was in the eighth grade. Her daughter's
squirrel face was without makeup, framed by a fluff of dark
hair. She was wearing a strawberry coat dress with big black
buttons up to her neck that was also a soft echo of Benny.

The desk was a standout, an executive model with
curving legs and no drawers that was probably as old as the
building.

"May I help you?" she asked.

"I hope so. I'm Freddie O'Neal, and I understand you

have a problem with my asking questions about Vince Marina's murder."

Her jaw dropped. She didn't know what to do with that. So I stood and waited.

"Not a problem," she finally said. "No, no, not a problem, there's no problem, certainly not. I'm sorry if when I talked to Sandra, she got the impression that there's any kind of problem, when there isn't. It's just—just—"

This is why I like to come in and ask questions without an appointment. If I'd called and let her know I was coming, she would have been prepared with what it "just" was.

I waited.

"It's just that Vince doesn't need a bodyguard anymore," Juanita said lamely, "now that he's dead. And since the authorities have already charged his ex-wife, and since she was, after all, the person you were supposed to protect him from, there doesn't seem to be much point in your being involved any longer. That's really all I wanted to say to Sandra."

"Oh, okay. Then since I don't believe Connie Marina offed her ex, and since I've been hired to make some inquiries, you don't have any problem with that, right?"

I watched her mind race around its cage. She was smarter than her brother, but she still didn't know what to do with this one. How to tell me to butt out without naming names.

"Well, if someone's hired you—"

"And it's not an open police investigation," I added.

"I suppose you have every right to ask questions."

The inflection of the sentence was chosen to make sure I understood that even though I had the right, she didn't think it was a good idea.

"Thanks. By the way, did you hear they dragged Tommy Durant out of the lake this afternoon?"

"No." That shook her. A lot. "No, I hadn't heard that. What happened?"

"He fell in and couldn't get out."

"I'm sorry. Oh, God, I'm sorry."

"Yeah. I am, too."

I left her there, sitting at her desk, her head in her hands.

If she told me what she knew, it would be because she couldn't live with it, not because I bullied her.

I took the drive back to Reno slowly, because I had nothing but cats waiting at the end of it and I wasn't sure what to do next. Somebody had to talk to me. If nobody talked, I was dead. Not literally. I hoped. Nobody talking really just meant that I took David Troy's money and failed to produce. The next best thing to dead.

The cats weren't on my front porch waiting. Arnie Lagatutta was.

"We gotta talk," he said.

"Okay. Come on in."

The office wasn't too bad. Everyone has piles of paper on their desks. I didn't want him to see the rest of the house.

"Can I get you something?"

I gestured toward one of the canvas chairs in front of the desk. Then I realized that wouldn't work. Arnie simply wouldn't have fit in one. He stood awkwardly.

"I'll take a beer," he said.

"Okay. Come on, we'll talk in the living room."

"Living room" is a misnomer. My office is in what was intended as the living room, so the room with the couch and two unmatched upholstered chairs was actually meant to be the second bedroom. The cats have clawed the couch, I've eaten dinner on it too many times, and what was once a not-bad burgundy has faded to Salvation Army brown. When Arnie sat on it, it sagged. Badly.

I went to the kitchen, hoping he wouldn't follow me, because it was really not meant for outside eyes. Or an outside nose. I had to remember to take the garbage out. Catfood cans piled up. I opened two bottles, took them back to the living room, handed one to Arnie, and sat in one of the chairs. I couldn't remember the last time I had sat in a chair instead of on the couch. I was a little surprised at how uncomfortable it was. But it really didn't matter a lot, because I couldn't remember the last time anyone else sat there, either.

"I want to know what you think happened to Tommy Durant," he said.

"I think he drowned."

"But you don't think it was an accident, and I want to know where you are."

"I think he drowned because somebody tied weights to his ankles."

His head bobbed in an odd way that I couldn't decipher as a nod or a shake.

"You think I did it?"

"I don't know. I think you're an obvious choice—a hired gun from L.A. who's asked to stick around for a few days when the reason for inviting him in the first place disappears."

"Would you believe me if I told you I didn't do it?"

"Try me."

"I didn't do it."

"Not quite good enough. Your eyes flickered. Either you did it or you know something about it."

Arnie stood up. He looked as if he wanted to pace, but the room was too small. He sat back down and swallowed a quarter of his beer.

"I didn't do it. I don't know for sure who did. I know who ordered it, and why, and I don't like what's going on, but there's really nothing I can do about it."

"Sure there's something you can do about it. We can walk over to the police station—it's less than a block away—and we can ask to see a detective, and you can tell him the story."

"Simple. You make it sound simple. Black and white. Right and wrong."

"That's what it is."

He shook his head.

"It's only simple for you because you're looking at it from the outside, you're not part of it, you don't have any loyalties. And I can tell you this—going to the police station might not help at all."

"Come on, Arnie, how bad is it. Craig Battaglia ordered Tommy killed because of his gambling debts, didn't he?" When Arnie didn't answer, I added, "More than that? I wondered why Battaglia didn't just bar him from the casino. You going to tell me?''

''Can't you just walk away from this one?'' The words came out like cannonballs, exploding in the room. ''If you're worried about Connie Marina, forget it. Probably there'll be a plea bargain, or if it does go to trial, the jury may not convict her. There are appeals, all kinds of things she can do to stay out of jail. She doesn't need you.''

''No, maybe not. But this isn't about Connie Marina—except that I think she's innocent and shouldn't have to face a trial or appeals or anything else. It's about a murdered man I was hired to protect. And it's about his murdered friend. And I guess it is about right and wrong. You've studied philosophy, you should understand the distinction.''

He smiled, a little.

''Want to go have dinner and talk philosophy? We could argue ethics—formalist versus utilitarian perspectives.''

''No. I don't. I've been out of school for too long to remember which is which. But it seems to me one of them has something to do with the common good. And I don't think either one lets you justify putting yourself first. I think *that* was Philosophy 102.''

''Yeah, maybe. Then I guess I gotta go. Thanks for the beer. And please, think about walking away from this one. Please.''

For a guy whose features had been rearranged a couple of times, Arnie had an expressive face. And he was begging me, really begging.

''I'll see you to the door,'' I said.

I opened another beer and sat in my office after he left, watching the afternoon light fade. Sundance jumped up on the window ledge, a bright splotch of orange against the twilight gray, and I let him in. Butch heard the door and was right behind him.

Arnie had wanted to scare me. I knew that. The thing was, he had succeeded. And the fact that he hadn't made any direct threat was more effective than if he had. That's what imagination is for—build your own threat, design your own consequences. If the big bad wolf tells you he'll huff and he'll puff and he'll blow your house down, you can reinforce your house. But if you don't know where he's coming from, or what he's likely to do, you start thinking of all the ways you're vulnerable, and you don't know where to start protecting yourself. I wasn't going to give up the case because of Arnie's unvoiced threats. But I wished I could. The more I sat there and thought about it, the worse I felt. I had to move.

I was feeling cold, so I pulled on a crewneck black wool sweater and a denim jacket before I left the house. A bit much for June, but I needed to feel protection from something, if only the evening chill. I also slipped a small gun into the pocket in the lining of my boot. I did this periodically, although I'd never used it, and I wasn't sure it would be much good if I had to. Guns small enough to fit in boots aren't very accurate and can't do much damage. I have a Beretta that I use for target practice, but it's a little heavy to carry around, and it invariably calls attention to itself.

I walked the few blocks to the Mother Lode in record time. I knew it was early to find Deke, but I figured I could wait for him. My fingers were crossed in my jacket pocket, a little sympathetic magic to support a hope that he wasn't doing something else for dinner.

Deke was there, at the counter. I felt absurdly relieved. Not because he could do anything to help, really. Just because he was there.

"Hey, Deke," I said, sliding in beside him. "You're here early."

He put down his coffee cup, leaned back at an angle that was almost too far for the stool, and fixed me with a fierce look from his red-rimmed eyes.

"So," he said. "You decided to stop by and tell your old friend what's going on. Finally."

"Yeah, I guess."

All of a sudden I didn't know what to tell him. I didn't want to say I was scared.

"How come you're drinking coffee?" I asked. "Did you eat already?"

"No. I waited. I was going to give you another fifteen minutes."

"Goddamn it, we didn't have a date or anything."

"Ah, yes, a date. One more surprise—not that your relationships are any of my business, of course."

"It wasn't exactly a date. I had to ask him about finding Vince Marina's body, and he said let's go to a movie, so I went. Not that it's any of your business."

"I can see there's a world of difference. You went to a movie, but it wasn't a date, because he's involved in the case you're working on. I gather that after our last discussion you decided to investigate Vince Marina's murder after all."

I was thinking about yelling at him, and almost sorry I'd been looking forward to seeing him, when Diane came down to our end of the counter and placed a beer in front of me.

"And a hamburger?" she asked.

"Yeah, thanks," I said.

Deke just nodded at her, and she nodded back. When you eat there as much as he does, a nod is an order.

"I do want to tell you what's going on," I said when Diane had left. "And it isn't about Arnie. Nothing's happening there. Believe me."

I told him about David Troy hiring me, Tommy Durant dying, and the rest, just sort of downplaying Juanita Elcano Holt and Arnie wanting me to quit.

"Maybe you should walk away from this one," Deke said when I was through.

"Why? Just because some thug suggested it?"

"No. Because the thug likes you, and he's afraid someone's going to want to hurt you, and he isn't going to be able to stop them."

"Last time we talked you said I ought to see it through."

"I changed my mind. You've learned enough to know that you couldn't have stopped Vince Marina's murder. And that was the reason I thought you should look into it. Now I think you should—do something else."

I filled out a Keno ticket, pulled out a dollar, and looked around for a runner.

"The word you were looking for was 'quit.' And the thing that disgusts me is you wouldn't have suggested quitting—you wouldn't even have talked around quitting—if I were a man. You would have said, 'A man's gotta do what a man's gotta do.' So don't ever say to me what you wouldn't say to a guy."

The new, young Keno runner picked up my ticket and my dollar.

"Good luck," she said, but this time it was a little automatic, and her smile looked a little tired.

Deke was waiting until I looked at him before he answered.

"You're almost right," he said. "There was a time I would have said that to a guy, and I wouldn't have heard how dumb it was. I used to say that all the time—I used to look at guys, guys who looked as white and pinched and scared as you did when you walked in here tonight, and say that to them. Nineteen-year-old boys with their first short haircut, I'd take them out in the desert and tell them what they had to do if they were going to survive. I'd lead them to the foot of a cliff and say they had to scale it. I'd point to a little jackrabbit and say they had to kill it and eat it if they wanted any dinner. And when they looked at me with eyes as sad and scared as the little jackrabbit's, I'd say, 'A man's gotta do what a man's gotta do.' And I don't do that no more. Now I think maybe the test of survival isn't so much what you can do on a mountainside or out on the desert. I think maybe it's just living your life the best you can and not getting in somebody's way when you don't belong there. So don't tell me what I would have said to a guy."

I hadn't realized I looked scared. But I knew I was sitting there, shoulders hunched, hugging myself, and that didn't exactly project an image of confidence.

"Okay, I'm sorry. And you're right, I'm scared. But I'm more scared of failing than I am of dying."

"Yeah, well, maybe you have to be over fifty before dying gets real to you. By then you've failed a couple times and lived through it. Then you be more scared of dying.''

''I'll let you know when I get there.''

We'd been caught together in a pool of cold tension that was suddenly sucked down a drain, leaving us still a little chilly, but relieved.

''So,'' Deke said, ''you're going to scale the cliff and kill the little jackrabbit.''

Oddly, that made me feel the job was doable after all.

''Yeah, I am.''

''Then maybe you ought to stay in touch. Just so I know how it's going.''

I looked up at the Keno board. I lost. It's a good thing I don't believe in omens, because I lose at Keno a lot.

''Yeah, sure.''

After dinner I walked back home, glad I had worn the sweater that seemed too heavy earlier. Once out of the neon haze, I could look up and see the stars. I was fed, warm, comfortable, and the threat might not be as real as it had felt with Arnie in the room. I could handle this.

David Troy had left a message on my answering machine, saying that he had a picture of Lisa for me, and asking how I wanted to get it. I called and told him I'd come up there in the morning.

I opened a beer and turned on the television set. I should have thought to pick up a movie. I watched until boredom and two sleeping cats knocked me out.

The photograph David Troy handed me showed a laughing woman nose to nose with Ricky's dog King, who also appeared to be having a good time. She had Vince's coloring, but her features were more delicate. Maybe not—his features had been pretty, too, before the dissipation started to show. In any case, this was the woman who had been standing with Craig Battaglia on the beach.

''Thanks,'' I said. ''This helps. Do you have any idea what Lisa's relationship with Craig Battaglia is?''

''Well, they're partners now, I suppose, after a fashion.''

''What?''

I lost my grip on the photograph, and had to scramble to keep it from landing in my coffee.

"Yes."

Troy's coffee had the strong, heady aroma that coffee acquires when a healthy shot of brandy has been added, and I almost wished I'd asked him to pour some in mine. He was well put together, in a white shirt, gray slacks, and a blue cardigan, but his eyes already had a skewed focus. He had greeted me alone. The Cadillac was parked in front, but not the Land Rover. Connie might have left with her son, might be simply indisposed.

"Vince owned a third of the Seraglio," he continued, sipping his aromatic coffee. "He left it to Lisa."

Hell. I knew I needed to ask about the will. And I had forgotten.

"How did Vince become part owner of the Seraglio? I thought the Battaglias owned the whole shebang."

"I don't know the details, of course. But apparently when Pete Battaglia wanted to expand from Reno to Lake Tahoe, about twenty years ago, he either had to borrow money or take a partner. He was averse to debt and chose to sell some of his equity—in this case, he sold a one-third interest in the corporation to Vince Marina."

"Why did he leave it to Lisa?"

"I imagine she wanted it. He left various other holdings to the other two children. Vince had invested his money, and he was well off when he died."

"Do you know what else was in his will?"

"I haven't seen a copy of it, if that's what you're asking. Ricky might have seen one. He and Connie have gone to Reno, to pick up Chris at the airport, and I don't know when they'll be back. If you want to ask him about it, you could try later. But from what I've heard, there were only a few bequests of personal items to old friends, and the rest went to the children."

"Nothing to Connie? Or to other women?"

"No, nothing to Connie. And I think I would have known if Vince had mentioned other women."

He smiled a little as he said it. I imagined what kind of

reaction Connie would have had and figured he was right. He would have known.

"Thanks for your help," I said. I finished my coffee and put the cup down. "I may be back later. I'll give you a call."

"Do you think you're getting anywhere, Miss O'Neal? Do you think you can prove someone other than Connie murdered Vince?"

"I don't know, Mr. Troy. But I'm doing the best I can."

He nodded, as if that was good enough for him, and walked me to the door.

The morning had been cool when I left Reno, but now it had warmed to maybe seventy. I tossed my jacket into the backseat of the Mustang. I wouldn't need it for the rest of the day.

The drive along the lake was becoming so familiar that I barely noticed how beautiful it was. I don't know that familiarity breeds contempt. But it does cause the special to appear shopworn.

I pulled into the Seraglio parking structure just before noon. Each time I looked for a place to park, I had to drive a little farther up the ramp. By August I'd be parking on the roof. In November, though, I could probably park on the street in front. I hoped I wouldn't still be driving up here in November.

I couldn't decide whether to try to catch Craig Battaglia before lunch, or eat first and try later. Hunger won the day. I walked the pedestrian bridge to the casino and negotiated the maze of smoky enchantments between the door and the coffee shop.

By the time I reached the hostess stand, I was walking a little faster, and I almost bumped into a woman in the black skirt and white blouse of a casino worker. We both stepped back in embarrassment when we recognized each other. I had almost smacked into Rita Mason.

"I was about to have lunch," she said. "You can join me if you want to."

"I do want to. Thanks."

We sat in a booth near the entrance. A waitress appeared immediately.

"Do you want coffee?" she asked.

We both nodded.

"And we'd like to order now," Rita added.

Looking at the menu did seem pointless. Rita ordered a chef's salad, I ordered bacon and eggs. The waitress poured our coffee and left.

"How're you doing?" I asked.

Rita shrugged.

"Okay. It seems I had already cried myself out over Vince—I couldn't cry when he died. And I don't know anything about it. That's what you want to ask, isn't it? Where was I the night he died?"

"Not unless you want to tell me. I believed you the first time, when you said you didn't want to kill him."

She added cream to her coffee.

"Then what do you want?"

"I believed Connie Marina, too, when she said she didn't kill him. So I'm trying to find out who else might have wanted him dead. And I was hoping you might have some information that would help."

"Like what?"

"I don't know. But I'm starting to think it might somehow be tied in to the Seraglio. Do you know anything about his connection here? Did he ever talk about it?"

"Come on. Vince never talked business with me. He did talk about the divorce—about Connie—but I don't know anything about his relationship with the Battaglias."

"But you knew he was a partner."

I took a sip of the coffee. It was my third cup of the day, and I was starting to feel jumpy.

"Sure. A lot of people knew that. They don't advertise it, but there was nothing secret about it."

"What about Lisa—Vince's daughter? Did you ever meet her?"

Rita laughed and shook her head. The laugh was thin, and twisted easily.

"That, of course, should have been a clue. Three nights

into what I thought was going to be a solid two weeks at the guest house, Lisa called and said she was on her way. He gave me an hour to get everything packed and out. Said I could come back when she left. She stayed for a week. I got the first three nights and the last three, but not even a word while Lisa was here.''

''I'm sorry.''

''It's okay. Not your fault I was dumb and in love.''

''Do you know if there's anything between Lisa and Craig Battaglia?''

''It's an interesting thought—and it would explain why she spent so much time here at the lake—but I've never seen them together.''

The food arrived. Rita attacked her chef's salad as if it were an enemy.

''What else do you want to know?'' she asked.

''Probably nothing you can tell me. Just how it all fits together.''

''You mean Tommy Durant?''

I had just picked up my fork, and almost dropped it.

''Yeah. You know something about that?''

''Not a thing.''

I wasn't sure I believed her. But that ended most of the conversation. We finished eating without either of us saying much more. I insisted on picking up the check, figuring it was a legitimate expense, and Rita left to go back to work—she had moved from swing to days, wasn't sure she liked the change because the tips weren't as good. I had another cup of coffee. If I was going to be jumpy, I might as well make it good.

It was not quite one o'clock when I took the elevator to the executive offices. I hadn't really expected Craig Battaglia to be there, but Monica buzzed him and received word to send me back.

This time he didn't stand up. He just sat there and waited.

''Lisa Marina,'' I said. ''Where do I find her?''

I had expected a show of surprise, or some sort of protest, but he didn't blink.

"I don't know where she is at the moment, and I wouldn't let you barge in on her in any event. I'll tell you what—I'm meeting her for dinner. I'll ask her if she wants to see you. If she does, she can call you tomorrow."

"It's important that I talk with her. I'd like a chance to tell her that. Also that her brother would like to talk with her."

"No problem. I'll tell her for you. And if that's all you wanted, I'd like to get back to work."

I could ask about the relationship, but he'd just say it was none of my business. And there was the possibility that it wasn't any of my business.

"It isn't all I wanted. I haven't heard from the *Odalisque* flight attendant, and I still need to talk with her, too. What did she say when you called her?"

He raised his eyebrows in mock surprise.

"I'm afraid it slipped my mind. I'll make a note so I don't forget again, and I'll call her this afternoon. I'm sure she'll get in touch with you if she has anything to say."

"Thanks for your help," I said.

"You're welcome."

We bared our teeth at each other and I left. I'd have to call Dean Sawyer to get in touch with the flight attendant, that was clear.

I waved to Monica, took the elevator back down, and crossed to the parking garage. I decided to drive back to the north shore and wait for Ricky Marina, to let him know where Lisa was and to check on the will. Then I could go home and try to sort it all out. I'd give Lisa Marina time to call me, although I didn't think there was much chance she would. Even if Battaglia gave her the message, she seemed to be part of the group that either thought her mother was guilty or wanted her to take the rap whether she was or not.

I noticed the gold limo in my rearview mirror shortly after I passed Zephyr Cove. But it was a couple of cars back, and it didn't really register until I made the left turn onto 28 and the limo followed. I slowed down to see if the driver was Andrew—I thought I'd honk and pull over if it was, see if he had something more to say to me. The limo slowed down, too, keeping its distance. All I could tell about the driver was that he was wearing dark glasses and a black cap. I picked up speed, and once again the limo followed suit. Well, if whoever it was wanted to follow me to Connie Marina's, that was okay. I was a little jumpy driving through the pines, but that was the coffee. And the isolation. It was the middle of the afternoon, the sun was shining, it was almost summer, and there ought to be other cars around.

I drove a little faster, wanting to get back to an inhabited area. For the first time in my life, I wanted to see the Ponderosa. The limo closed the distance. This was nuts, of course. I couldn't be in danger from someone in a gold limousine in the middle of a bright afternoon. I put a little pressure on the accelerator, and the Mustang's rebuilt engine responded. The rolling hills of pine trees swept by, and I could see the lake again. The limo dropped back, and I slowed down. The cars passed, going the other way.

And the limo was suddenly on my tail. I hit sixty, then eighty, found myself almost on top of a red Chevy, pulled left to pass on a curve, and barely made it back to the right lane before a black Honda, horn screaming and brakes screeching, landed where I had been. The limo was gone, but I kept it at eighty, hands damp on the steering wheel, praying the highway patrol had a car wandering around the north shore.

Two curves later the gold limo found me again. I went to a hundred and ten, and the limo stayed with me. Houses—we were passing houses on the right, a cliff down to the lake on the left. But Lakeshore Drive was coming up on the left, the road down to the water. If I swerved at the last minute and braked right before the turn from the left-hand lane—and if there were no cars coming in that lane—I could make the turn, and the limo couldn't.

I held steady until I was almost at the spot where Lakeshore Drive wound down from the highway to the beachfront houses. Then I pulled over into the wrong lane and hit the brakes, hoping I could slow down enough to make the turn.

I think I could have made it, too. But the limo didn't try to follow. The driver neatly clipped my right rear fender as I started the turn at eighty miles an hour. I felt the car leave the road, felt it start to float out over the cliff, saw a dizzy, whirling, flashing blue that could be either sky or lake.

I know they tell you you're safer staying in the car in case of an accident. The worst things happen when you're thrown clear, or when you jump. But I panicked, and I had to get out of there. I never learned to swim very well, and the worst fear in my life is drowning. So I pushed open the door and fell out of the car, tumbled through the air, all the time thinking how stupid this was, that nobody in a gold limo runs you off the road in bright daylight. I hit something, and hurt all over, and then I didn't feel anything more.

The cold woke me up. The cold and the pain. I lay there, drowning in pain colder than ice water, not sure if consciousness was a state I wanted. But the pain and the cold demanded my attention. The pain seemed to be emanating from my left temple. The cold was all over. I had a faint memory of tossing my jacket in the backseat when I got into the car, thinking I wouldn't need it. Maybe, if I was lucky, the car had landed close enough that I could get the jacket back. I was going to have to open my eyes to look for it.

I opened my eyes into darkness. The fall had knocked me out of the day, and the reason I was cold was that the sun was down. It was night in the mountains, and I was wearing nothing but a light shirt with my jeans. I started testing muscles, to see what worked and what didn't before I moved. Everything seemed okay. I sat up—too swiftly—I had to shut my eyes again and swim through the pain in my head. I used my hands, feeling my body, to assess the damage. My shirt was torn, and my skin as well. But I was fairly certain that I had no injuries beyond scrapes and bruises. I realized that I was leaning against a tree, and I used it as a crutch, to hoist myself up.

The trees must have broken my fall. That would explain the abrasions, and the fact that apparently nothing was broken. It would also have hidden me, so that no one driving along the road could have seen me, all the time I was out.

Once up, once oriented, I could see a little. I could see stars, and the sky, above the tree. And where the road was. I couldn't see my car, which had to be somewhere down toward the water, or in the water. Shivering, I started toward the road.

Probably the sensible thing would have been to head for the nearest house on Lakeshore Drive and ask the people who lived there to call the police. But I was cold and aching and frightened and I didn't think to do that. I knew where I was going, about two miles down the road and half a mile up to the right. And I was certain I could make it. One step at a time. I focused on my feet, on moving them. Sometimes, when I thought about it, I wiggled my fingers and rubbed my arms, where I was hugging myself, holding myself together. One step at a time.

Headlights whipped by, and I thought maybe I should be standing with my thumb out, but I was afraid if I stopped I couldn't start moving again. The cold would close over my head, and I would drown in the cold. One step and then the next. One step at a time, that's how I would get there. I listened to the crunch of my boots in the dirt beside the road. That was comforting, the rhythm, the steady sound of my boots. I listened, and I looked for the road that I would take up the hill.

I was almost at the door before I realized that I had started to climb. I didn't remember turning, but some sort of instinct must have clicked in. The house was a smaller version of Connie Marina's, two stories of cedar and a steep roof. A gray Oldsmobile and a blue Toyota Forerunner were parked in the gravel drive, and the porch light was on. I felt a flood of warmth when I closed my hand around the brass knocker. It ebbed a little when no one answered, when I had to pound on the door. I didn't know how late it was. Maybe nobody was awake.

Finally, the door cracked, held against a chain. I heard a woman gasp. The chain slipped, the door opened, and a short, slender, fiftyish woman with bright red hair curling about her shoulders, dressed in a lavender-and-turquoise silk kimono, whispered, "My God! Freddie, what's happened?"

"Hi, Mom," I said, slumping against the door frame.

I think Robert Frost said it: "Home is the place where, when you have to go there, they have to take you in."

Chapter 8

THE SHOUTING WOKE me up. Just like old times. Mom and Al shouting at each other, arguing about me. I couldn't hear the words, but I knew the tune. He was saying that he'd done enough for me, and he didn't want me around. She was saying that I was her daughter, and she wanted me around for as long as I wanted to stay, which probably wouldn't be very long anyway. Or something like that.

Once she got over the shock of my arrival the night before, Mom had run a bath for me, fixed a pot of tea, and loaned me one of Al's bathrobes, a really soft navy-blue job that I considered walking off with. He probably wouldn't wear it again, once he found out I'd borrowed it, and there was no sense letting it go to waste.

I had shivered in the hot tub for a long time, with the electric wall unit on high. The cold had penetrated past skin and muscle, all the way to bone, and at first I was afraid it would never crack.

When I got out of the tub, the tea was waiting, and so was Mom. I didn't drink very much tea, because I got sleepy immediately. She had wanted to know what happened, and I just told her about the accident, not the case. That was what I said, a car accident. You don't tell your mother that somebody tried to kill you by forcing your car off the cliff. Besides, for a few moments, I wanted to feel safe, and I knew that talking about what happened would scare me all over again. She tucked me in and went back to bed with Al.

The shouting stopped. I was glad, because I didn't want to walk into it when I went downstairs, which I would have to do sooner or later. I knew it was late morning, because the sun was shining through the lace priscillas, left over from the brief period several years before when this was officially "my room." I needed a cup of coffee, and then I needed to get back to my car. If I still had one.

First, I needed to move. My right eyelid worked, but the left one was too swollen to get above half-staff. I might have to avoid mirrors for a while. My left shoulder was sore, also an area above my left kidney. I could almost remember bumping my way down the tree, back by shoulder by forehead. I eased out of bed and into Al's bathrobe. I was a little dizzy at first, but I wasn't seeing double, and I decided I didn't have a concussion. There was no sign of my clothes, or what was left of them.

I had to use the bathroom, and that meant a mirror.

The bruise was centered toward the outside of my left cheekbone. It was already dark purple. That meant I could look forward to varying shades of green and yellow for the next two weeks. The color and the swelling gave me new insight into why a black eye is called a mouse. I splashed some cold water on my face, which made me feel a little better, but didn't help my appearance. Borrowing Mom's hairbrush helped a little, but nothing was going to make me look good.

The ground floor of the house was one very large room, with a living area, a dining area, and an open kitchen. The south wall, looking out over the lake, was all glass. I was getting so used to picture-postcard vistas that I barely glanced at it.

Mom was sitting at the table, again in her kimono. Al was standing in the kitchen, pouring himself a mug of coffee. He turned when he heard my footsteps. I could tell from his glare that the bathrobe was a goner. Into the fireplace the minute I left.

"Al has agreed to drive you back to the place you went off the road and help you with your car," Mom said loudly, with a steely undertone, telling him he'd better not start again. Then she got a look at my face, and hers went soft. "But I think you ought to see a doctor first. We know one in Incline Village, and I'm certain that under the circumstances he'd squeeze you in this morning."

"Thanks, but I really think I'm okay. And Al doesn't need to drive me, although I'd appreciate it if I could borrow the Toyota."

"Of course Al will go with you. He wouldn't dream of letting you go alone."

Al and I looked at each other, trying to decide which would be worse, riding together or arguing with Mom.

"Mind if I get a cup of coffee?" I asked.

"Help yourself," he answered, moving out of my way.

Al wasn't a bad guy. He was tall and fat and sincere, with a few gray hairs on top of his shiny head, and a full gray mustache. He had made enough money as a real-estate developer that he could opt for early retirement. As far as I knew, he spent his days sitting on the deck, staring at the water, enjoying his idleness. It was because of Al that I owned my own home—he had picked it up cheap at a foreclosure and negotiated a loan that I could make payments on. I would always like him a little because of that, no matter what else he had done to make my life miserable.

He watched me limp to the coffeepot.

"Your mother's right, you should see a doctor," he said. "Your face looks pretty ugly and you're not walking very well."

"Yeah, I know, but I think the damage is external, and however awful I look, I ought to heal. Besides, I hate doctors."

"Up to you. You're a big girl."

My hand tensed around the coffeepot. Al could rub me the wrong way faster than anyone in the world.

"Where're my clothes? I'd like to check out the car as soon as possible."

"Well, you'll have to wait," Mom said. "I threw that shirt away, but I washed your jeans, and they're still in the dryer. You can borrow one of Al's sweatshirts."

Al and I looked at each other again.

"You can have one," he said. "I'll pick one out and leave it on your bed."

He took his coffee mug upstairs with him. I was betting it would take him until my jeans were dry to decide which sweatshirt to give me.

"Come sit with me," Mom said.

I obeyed, on cue.

"I don't want the speech about getting along with Al. It's not going to happen."

"Oh, I know. I wasn't going to give you that one at all—I want to give the one about your being too smart to be in a dangerous business, one where you get hurt."

She reached over and brushed my hair back off my forehead. There were two things that always amazed me about Mom: one was how lovely she looked, how clear and unlined her skin still was, even in the morning, with no makeup on. The other was her ability to turn me into an infant with one simple gesture. Resisting the impulse to let her take me over, I bristled.

"I didn't say the accident had anything to do with a case."

"No, you didn't. But you've been driving without an accident since you were fourteen, and you loved that Mustang. If you wrecked it, someone forced you to. And that means someone wanted to hurt you. I really wish you were making a living some other way."

"Goddamn it, where are my jeans?"

I had to get out of there, or I was going to start crying. The washer and dryer were in a small room that connected the main house with the garage. I turned off the dryer and tested my jeans. They were still a little damp around the zipper, but I could live with that. I grabbed my underwear—which she had thoughtfully pulled out of the dryer and hung on a rack—and marched painfully back through the kitchen and up the stairs.

Al had picked a UNLV sweatshirt—his alma mater. I was sure he had done it on purpose, knowing I'd never wear it again. I pulled on my jeans and his sweatshirt and looked for my boots. They were standing neatly at the end of the bed, the gun still in its pocket. Jesus. I was lucky I hadn't blown my ankle off.

Mom was waiting at the table when I came back down the stairs.

"I wasn't through, you know," she said quietly.

"I just can't listen to it. This is the only thing I know how to do. I wouldn't be happy doing anything else. And I'm sorry it makes you unhappy."

Her mouth got tight, like she didn't want to cry in front of me. Mom and I were great at not wanting to cry in front of each other.

"I hope your car's all right," she said.

"Thanks."

Al was standing at the front door, car keys in hand.

"I'd really rather go alone," I said.

He nodded.

"And I'd let you."

He opened the door, walked out, got into the Toyota, and started it. I had to follow or walk back to my car, and I couldn't handle that. I settled uncomfortably into the passenger seat.

Al drove like an old man, shoulders hunched, neck strained, hands gripping the steering wheel at high noon. But he'd driven that way when he was forty. Riding with him had always made me nervous. He jerked to a stop at the highway, peered cautiously both ways, eased a couple of feet farther, jerked to another stop, and peered again.

"Which way?"

"South, a couple of miles. When you get to the Lake-shore Drive turnoff, pull over and park."

He waited for a car that was about half a mile away to pass, and then turned onto the highway so slowly I was glad he'd waited. I shut my eyes until I felt the tires move from asphalt to dirt. Watching Al was only going to raise my blood pressure, and anyway, my left eye was hurting.

"I don't see your car," he said.

I couldn't see it either. I got out and looked at the road. There were skid marks that had to be mine, from my futile effort to keep the car on the road. I followed them to the edge and looked over. I still couldn't see it. I started down the hill, ignoring the throb in my head.

"How're you going to get back up?" Al called.

"The same way I did last night," I yelled back.

I spotted a tree with a broken branch that was probably responsible for the bruise over my left kidney and stayed to the right of it. I didn't have to go much farther before I could see the Mustang. It must have landed once or twice and bounced, because it was upside down, trunk in the water, engine partly hidden by a rock. Waves lapped gently where the back window had been, swirling around the crushed backseat. The windshield was gone, too. If I hadn't looked for the car, it might have rotted there. And if I hadn't jumped, I might have rotted with it. One more body on the beach.

I sat down where I was, back against a tree, and started to sob. I know it was just a car, and cars don't have lives the way animals do, but all I could think of was a racehorse with a broken back that would have to be destroyed. The car couldn't have fallen that far, ended up like that, without chassis damage. It was junk now. And I had loved it as much as I had loved anything in my life.

"Are you okay?" Al shouted down at me.

I wasn't okay, but there wasn't any point in saying so, because there was nothing Al could do about it.

"I can see the car, I'll be a few minutes," I answered.

"What?"

I repeated it, louder.

I needed to think about what came next, and I hurt too much to think clearly. I leaned my head against my knees.

There was no reason to go all the way down to the car. I couldn't do anything to help it—I probably couldn't even get my jacket out, given the angles and the water—and the climb back up would be that much harder. There also wasn't any reason to report it to the police, at least not yet. If anyone had seen the car go off the road, I would have been found. And I couldn't face making a report to some desk sergeant, trying to explain that a gold limo ran me off the road in the middle of the afternoon. I would have to talk to the police sooner or later, and my insurance company, but I would try to put it off until some of the deeper issues were resolved. So I could prove the gold limo ran me off the road.

I felt a little better. I stood up and climbed back up to the road, only stumbling a couple of times.

"The Mustang's totaled," I said. "And I need a car. I'll understand if you don't want to lend me the Toyota, but could you drive me someplace where I could rent something?"

Al had to think about it. Finally he held out his hand, car keys dangling.

"Thanks, Al. I appreciate this, I really do."

It took me about two minutes to drive Al back to the house. He shut his eyes when I made a U-turn on the highway, and didn't open them until I paused in the gravel drive.

"What do you want me to tell Ramona?" he asked.

"Tell her I'm going to go home and feed my cats, and I'll call her later."

"Drive carefully."

"I will. Thanks again."

We almost smiled at each other.

Actually, I did want to go home and feed my cats. But I didn't want to drive back to Reno without checking the will. I would just have to come right back. So even though I didn't feel like explaining my face to anyone, not just then, I turned right at the highway, toward Crystal Bay.

The Toyota drove like a truck, and I missed the Mustang. I started crying again.

I stopped at a drugstore and bought a pair of wraparound sunglasses. I was going to buy cheap ones, but then I decided they were a chargeable expense. They didn't completely hide the swelling on the left side of my face, but they were the best I could do.

There were three cars parked in the gravel in front of Connie Marina's house. Wence was there again.

David Troy answered my knock. He raised a polite eyebrow when he saw my face.

"Are you all right, Miss O'Neal? Has something happened?"

"It's okay, Mr. Troy. I was in an accident, that's all. I'm sorry to barge in on you, but you told me Ricky might have seen a copy of Vince's will, and I'd like to talk with him about it."

"He's here. You can ask him, if you wish. Although I'd appreciate it if you formed the habit of calling before coming over."

He stepped back, and I followed him into the living room. Connie and Ricky were sitting on the couch, with King at Ricky's feet. Roland Wence was standing near the bar. A man with a strong family resemblance to Ricky and Connie, but darker, was staring out the window. Troy introduced him as Chris Marina, Vince's other son, and explained my presence to the group. I did my best to stay in the shadows by the door, and no one said anything about my face. Nobody even noticed it. Whatever had been going on before I arrived had coated everyone in the room with a shiny glaze of tension.

"I don't have a copy of the will," Ricky said, trying to smile at me, "but Dad's attorney told me that he left everything to his kids. I just haven't been concerned about what I was going to get."

"I'm sure you haven't—and I'm sorry—but maybe you could ask for a copy. It might be important who gets what, like Lisa getting the interest in the Seraglio."

"What the hell difference does it make?" Chris turned from the window, spitting out words like shrapnel. "You can't get Mom off by dragging us in."

"No, and I don't want to do that. But Lisa *is* in, because she was at the guest house that night, and she's staying at the Seraglio, and she doesn't seem to be communicating with the rest of the family."

Connie picked up the phone, yelled at the information operator, punched out a number, and handed the receiver to Ricky.

"You ask for her," she said.

He did, but looked puzzled at the response.

"She isn't registered," Ricky said, turning to me.

"Ask for Craig Battaglia."

We waited while the call was transferred.

"Hey, Craig, it's Ricky. I heard Lisa was hanging out at the Seraglio, and I really need to talk to her. Can you help?" Pause. "No, come on. She meant Mom, she didn't mean me." Pause. "This just doesn't cut it. Lisa doesn't need you as a mediator. You're only making things worse. Tell her that—and that sooner or later she's going to have to talk to me."

He clicked off the phone.

"Craig says she hates us all and doesn't want to see any of us."

"Give me the keys to the Land Rover," Chris said, closing the distance to the sofa in two steps. "If she's at the Seraglio, I'll find her."

Ricky picked them up from the coffee table and held them out.

"Drive carefully."

Something happened between the brothers that was almost warm and caring, but it was gone instantly. Chris brushed past me and out the door.

"I'll follow him to the Seraglio," I said. "I was going that way anyway."

"Should we assume that you have nothing further to report?" Roland Wence asked.

"Not at this time, Mr. Wence."

"I see. Well then, Miss O'Neal, you, too—drive carefully."

Wence was smiling as he said it. I didn't want to get paranoid here, so I just smiled back and said good-bye.

Every muscle screamed in protest as I turned the car toward South Shore. My body wanted to go the other way, over Mount Rose and home to a hot bath and a couple of cats that had probably foraged dinner and breakfast to supplement their bowl of dried food. At the same time, though, I needed to find Lisa Marina. And I wanted to check the row of gold limos for one with a dented fender.

I drove so carefully that I didn't catch up with Chris. But

I did cruise the Seraglio garage until I found the Land
Rover, then parked where I could watch it. In my physical
state, I wasn't going to be able to run all over the hotel
looking for anybody. They would have to come to me. I
figured I had just enough energy to get to the basement and
back.

The limo I was looking for might not have been there, of
course. It could have been at the airport, or off on a jaunt
with some VIP, or simply hidden. But since they didn't
think anyone would be looking for it, it was right in plain
sight. There were four gold limos against the far wall of the
basement. And one had a crumpled left front fender. I
needed a picture of it, showing the license plate. The picture
wouldn't be proof, but it might help. My camera was in the
trunk of the Mustang.

The pain in my back was worse, my legs were wobbly,
and I was beginning to be aware of my stomach protesting
that all I had consumed for a long time was last night's tea
and this morning's coffee. As I trudged from the garage to
the hotel gift shop—the camera was a chargeable expense,
and I couldn't go any further—I felt as if I was walking
toward a mountain on the horizon, one that receded with
every mile I advanced. I could understand how early
desert-crossers went nuts in their Conestogas, seeing the
Sierras get farther away as they moved forward.

The shop was one of several just off the lobby. Actually,
the real gift shop had a lot of heavy jewelry that looked a lot
cheaper than it was and some pricey ceramic ware. The one
I wanted was closer to a drugstore, with little bits of this and
that, paperback best-sellers and magazines on one wall,
toothpaste and deodorant on another. There were only a
couple of cameras, both Japanese. Not many tourists come
to the lake to take pictures, or if they do, they bring their
own cameras. I pointed out to the clerk that the lack of an
American-made alternative was forcing me to add to the
trade deficit, but she just looked puzzled. I bought the
smaller of the two 35-millimeter jobs and a roll of Fuji film.

Standing in the doorway, I weighed my choices. I could
go to the coffee shop and risk missing Chris Marina. Or I

could return directly to the car and faint from lack of food. I turned back to the counter and bought a chocolate bar.

Then came the painful trek back through the lobby, made slightly easier because this time I had provisions. Saliva gushed into my mouth as I crumpled the paper wrapper and tossed it in an ashcan. I peeled back the foil and took a bite of the dark chocolate, pausing so that I wouldn't get dizzy from the sugar rush. My stomach growled in outrage, having hoped for a hamburger, but at least it had something to work on.

If there is such a thing as a panacea, chocolate is the first ingredient, and fat probably the second. The candy bar even seemed to help my sore muscles.

As I left the lobby the garage receded to the horizon for a moment, but I focused my eyes and brought it back. I crossed the drive and limped down the ramp to the basement.

The gold limo was gone. Where there had been four, side by side against the back wall, only three remained. And I hadn't even written down the license plate.

"Were you looking for me, Miss O'Neal?"

The voice made me jump. Andrew had appeared from somewhere, and stood beside me in his uniform, cap in hand.

"Not really, but maybe you can help. The other limo—the one with the smashed fender—where has it gone and who was driving it?"

"I'm not aware of a dented fender on any of the limousines. There was another car here, true. There are five in all—one has just returned from the airport, it's in front of the hotel now, and I imagine the fifth has been sent on an errand. I have no idea who might be driving it, because there are only four regular drivers, and we were all having lunch when Matthew was sent to the airport. The other two are still in the coffee shop."

"Four drivers, five limos?"

Andrew nodded solemnly.

"We refer to the extra limo as the 'fifth wheel.' Like a spare tire, it's there in case something goes wrong with one of the regular four. You might check with Mr. Battaglia. He might have taken it on some personal business.''

"Does anyone else have the authority to take it?''

"Yes—Mr. d'Azevedo, head of security.''

My two best buddies.

"Andrew, suppose for a moment that there *was* a dented fender on the extra limo, the fifth wheel. Where would they take it to get it fixed?''

"Reno—Carroll's Body Work, on East Second.''

"Thanks.''

I started up the ramp, moving as carefully as I could, trying vainly to keep my weight off my legs.

"Are you all right, Miss O'Neal?'' Andrew called.

"Yeah. Had a little accident, but I'm all right.''

I was less all right when I got back to the Toyota and realized that the Land Rover, too, had disappeared in my absence. I tossed the camera onto the passenger seat and started crying again. The bruises on my ego felt even worse than the ones on my body. I felt like a failure. For all I knew, Chris had found Lisa and they were on the way to Crystal Bay. Sometime I would have to call and find out, confessing to David Troy that I had lost Chris, but not right then. And I knew I couldn't drive there to check before going home. I just didn't have the strength.

Nothing happened on the drive home to cheer me up. I had to take it slowly, due to pain, exhaustion, and the unfamiliar Toyota. The hamburger I picked up at a drive-thru in Carson City made me sluggish, and I dripped sauce on both my jeans and the car seat, which would not endear me to Al.

I parked in the driveway and dragged myself to the house. A pile of feathers and one identifiable dove's wing were right inside the front door. That was okay—doves were dumb birds anyway. I could clean it up later.

Sundance streaked through the door before I had a chance to close it, further scattering feathers on his way to the kitchen. Butch was sitting on my desk, where he had spread the papers around so that he was comfortable, looking at me reproachfully.

"I'm sorry you were reduced to hunting," I told him. "Come on, I'll open a can."

I braced myself against the wall of the bathroom as I leaned over and started the tub. I don't usually take baths, so I had to wait for the spurt of rust to clear before I put the plug in. Flopping down on the bed was what I wanted to do most, but common sense argued for a bath first, to relax my back muscles.

As I stepped into the kitchen something crunched under my left boot. A long, thin, hairless tail stuck out from the side. I lifted my boot, but the tail came with it. I put my foot back down. I was standing on the uneaten asshole of a rat. You have to be a real failure to lose your client, lose your car, lose the guy you were following, and then step on a rat's asshole on your own kitchen floor.

I was too depressed to cry anymore. I cleaned off the bottom of my boot, put a can of food down for the cats so there wouldn't be any more incidents for a while, got into the tub, and lay there until the water got cold. The phone rang, but I didn't move.

Everything could go to hell for all I cared.

Chapter
9

I ROUSED ONCE in the night, when I tried to turn over and couldn't, because I was pinned down by the two cats. They readjusted themselves grudgingly, and I slipped back down into the pool of my pain.

The phone rang again, sometime early in the morning, and I ignored it. Sooner or later I would have to check messages, but not yet.

The problem with bruises and muscle strains and other such minor injuries is that you don't always realize right away how bad they are. You keep going with shock or adrenaline or something and then all of a sudden you can't move. That Saturday morning, one week to the day from Vince Marina's murder, I woke up paralyzed.

Well, okay. I wasn't literally paralyzed. But electric prods were attached to the top and bottom of my spine, and they weren't activated unless I tried to move. As long as I was flat and motionless, they were inert. When I lifted my head, the voltage shot down. Bending a knee caused an upward jolt.

There was no way I could survive without food, water, and help. I reached for the phone, carefully, without moving more than my arm, and punched Deke's number.

"I'm home. Can you come over?" was about all I could get out. He hung up. I went back to sleep until I heard him kick the door open. I forgot I had slipped the chain. I would have to replace it with something better.

I heard his footsteps coming down the hall to the bedroom.

"Shit. What happened?"

I told him.

"Okay. I'll carry you to the car, and we'll get them to X-ray you at Washoe Medical, just to make sure there're no internal injuries."

"No way. I hate doctors. And it's just muscles, I know it's just muscles."

"How do you know?"

"No blood," I said. "No blood from any orifice, and I don't feel sick. Just hurt. If I were really in trouble, there'd be some sign by now."

He backed off a little at the mention of blood. Men are real squeamish about blood.

"Let's roll you over," he said. "If your spine feels all right—no exploding disks—I'll go along. Otherwise, we go to the hospital."

The bad part was rolling me over. By then I hurt so much that I couldn't even feel his hands running down my spine. The electric prod was humming in my ears.

"Nothing out of line. You were lucky—one more time. But you may be like this for a week."

"Oh, God, Deke. I can't be."

I said it into the pillow, and had to say it again after he rolled me back over.

"I have to get up—please. Please get me something that will help."

He looked at me, shut his red-rimmed eyes, and shook his head.

"Why do you have to get up today?"

"I have to check the garage to see if the gold limo is there. I should have done it yesterday. Probably the fender has already been fixed."

"I can check the garage. Better me than you anyway—somebody might be there who doesn't want to see you well and happy. What else that can't wait?"

I couldn't come up with anything.

"I'll be back in a little while. Don't move."

That would have been funny, except I had to pee. I waited until I heard him slam the door before I tried to get up. The electric prod started shooting from both sides, and I decided standing was out. Crawling would get me there. As I pulled myself up onto the toilet I considered stopping to vomit, but I knew there was nothing to come up. I got back to bed just in time to pass out again.

With no chain to break, Deke returned quietly. What woke me this time was the smell of soup. A large mug was steaming on my bedside table.

"I took your garbage out," he said, "because it was the only way I could stand to be in your kitchen long enough to heat this up. I ain't gonna do your dishes or clean up what's left of that bird."

"Thanks. What happened at the garage?"

"Let's prop you up a little first so you can start on the soup."

He had grabbed the cushions from my couch and managed to arrange those under the pillows so my body was angled enough that I could sip from the mug. But he handed me a glass of water first and held out two small green tablets.

"Here, take these."

"What?"

"They're prescription muscle relaxers—I keep them around for when my back goes out."

"Thanks again. So what happened at the garage?"

I swallowed the tablets, discovered I was dehydrated, and drank the rest of the water. Deke took the glass and gave me the mug. He sat down on the edge of the bed.

"I drove my car in, told them I wanted an estimate on getting the dings knocked out. And sure enough, the gold limo was there, but no dented fender. Looked cherry. So when the guy gave me the estimate, I told him it was high, wasn't worth it—which was true. He started arguing about how good he was, and I steered him over to the gold limo, and he told me all about how he had fixed it yesterday on a rush job, and nobody could see where it had been bad. I went, 'My, my, you sure are good at your job,' and he told me the rest, how d'Azevedo had brought it in, needed to pick it back up Monday, and since the paint needed two days to dry, he'd had to get right at the fender.''

"Did he tell you what happened to the fender?"

"D'Azevedo said a new driver had clipped the post at the entrance to the garage. No reason to doubt him.''

"Shit. There isn't a new driver.''

"I know. Anything else you need? I was just falling asleep when you called this morning, and if you're okay for a while, I need to take a nap.''

Deke stretched out his shoulders as he stood up. I felt bad for not remembering—I knew he usually went to bed about ten in the morning, and it must have been about eleven when I called.

"Could I ask for one more thing?"

"If it's short.''

"Check my answering machine?"

"I'd say no, because you need to forget about working today, but I'm afraid you'd just try to get down the hall to your office on your belly like a snake.''

I closed my eyes until I heard him come back.

"Your mother called, worried. Sandra called. There were two hang-ups. And David Troy called to say that Lisa is staying at the guest house.''

"Shit. Of course. The comedian who took over for Vince isn't going to want to stay there, so somebody might as well. Damn, damn, I ought to get up there to talk to her.''

"You ought to call your mother and then sleep for a couple of days. I'll refill your water glass and your soup mug, and then I'll be over with some chicken or something later. You gonna be all right alone for a while?"

"Yeah, sure. And thanks, a lot. I keep saying thanks, and it sounds dumb, but I mean it.''

"If you want to thank me, you stay in bed.''

I reached out and took his hand, but that embarrassed both of us. When I heard Deke lock the front door, I picked up the phone. He was right. I had to call Mom.

I apologized for not having called her sooner, told her I'd

been sleeping. I could hear Al in the background, saying, "Ask her when she's going to bring the car back."

Mom snapped "Hush!" at him. That always used to shut me up, and it stopped Al, too.

"Tell Al I'll get the car back sometime next week. And tell him thank you."

"Are you sure you're all right?"

"Yeah. I'll call you soon."

There wasn't anything I could do about David Troy or the hang-ups, but I could call Sandra. I had to think about how much I wanted to tell her. I decided on everything. At this point, I needed all the help I could get.

"I've been leaving messages for *days*," she said. "I called as soon as I heard about Tommy Durant. What's happening?"

I filled her in on the little I knew about Tommy, my conversation with Juanita Elcano Holt, and my mishap with the limo. And assured her I was all right.

"What can I do?" she asked.

"I'm not sure. Maybe you could work on the Carson City connection, push your friend Juanita a little. Make it sound as if I'm near death, that sort of thing."

"No—I meant for you. Do you need food?"

That's the one consolation of being hurt. Everybody offers to bring you food. Nobody does that when you're okay.

"Thanks, but Deke is taking care of me tonight, and I expect to be up and about tomorrow."

"I'll stop by in the morning and make sure."

"What about Carson?"

"First thing Monday."

I had stayed propped on the sofa cushions, and I didn't feel like moving off them. It was just enough of an angle that I could watch television. I clicked on the remote and ran though the available channels until I found an old John Wayne movie. *Hondo*—one of the "a man's gotta do" movies. The one where Geraldine Page tells him that a man's got his work, but all a woman's got is her man. Of course, she's been running the ranch and raising a son alone, and doing okay, but I guess that doesn't count. I would have liked her better if she'd worn less lipstick.

Deke's pills were starting to work, and I was feeling almost comfortable and a little drowsy when I heard somebody come in the front door. The footsteps were a little heavy, but I figured Deke was carrying something.

Arnie walked into the bedroom.

"Don't you knock?" I yelled, trying to sit straight up, and having to give up the idea when the electric prods went off again.

"I'm sorry. I heard you were hurt, and when I walked around the house, the only sounds of life were from the bedroom, and I didn't want to get you up. I needed to know if you're okay. I guess you're not."

I tried to hide the bruised side of my face in the pillow.

"It's not as bad as it looks."

"Yeah, sure. Listen, you gotta get a new lock for your door. It's not safe, I opened it with a credit card. And your chain's busted, I guess you know that. And there are feathers—"

I whipped my head around so fast it made my back hurt.

He held up his hands in a gesture of surrender.

I clicked off Gerry and the Duke and pointed to the foot of the bed.

"Sit down and tell me what you know."

"I'll tell you what I *can*." Arnie was clearly unhappy about telling me anything at all. "Chris Marina stormed the Seraglio offices yesterday, demanding to know where his sister was staying. The receptionist got scared, and said she was in the dining room having lunch with Battaglia. There was a big argument. Brother and sister left together. Battaglia asked d'Azevedo why the girl dick—sorry—was still in action. And d'Azevedo said he thought you were taken care of, but he'd check it out. I said I'd do it for him. I called, but there was no answer. I came down here, but nobody was home. I thought I'd try again."

"To finish me off?"

"Come on, Freddie, no, not to finish you off." Arnie stood up, but there still wasn't any room to pace, so he sat back down. "Tell me what happened. Then we can figure out what I can report."

"Oh, hell. Why should I trust you?"

"Because you didn't take my advice and get out of this. Now you gotta trust me."

His eyes were wide and round and almost innocent. And he was right. I had to trust him.

I told my tale one more time. Except I said a friend's house, not my mother's. I didn't trust him quite that much.

At the end, he nodded.

"Okay. I'll say you're hurt bad, and you're in hiding. Hurt bad is true, and hiding is where you ought to be."

He raised his eyebrows hopefully. The expression was clownish. I shook my head.

"This is where I live," I said, "and I'm not leaving."

"Okay."

I was relieved, if a little surprised, that he hadn't argued with me.

"But you can't leave the Toyota in the driveway," he continued. "I'll move it for you before I go. And you need to beef up security. I'll put a dead bolt on the front door and check the window locks. As a temporary measure, we might want to nail some of the windows shut. Do you have a gun?"

"Yes. And here's where we stop for a while. Nothing changes until Deke gets back."

His expression didn't alter.

"When's that?"

"Soon. He didn't tell me what time. I can call him and ask."

"Just call him and tell him I'm moving the Toyota so he won't get scared when it isn't in front. While you're doing that I'll take a look at windows and doors."

Arnie glanced briefly at the two bedroom windows and walked out. I dialed Deke's number and got the answering machine. I waited for the beep.

"Hey, Deke," I said, doing my best to sound as if someone was at the other end. "Arnie's here, and he thinks I'm not secure enough. He wants to move the car and put a dead bolt on the front door, and a couple of other things.''

I paused for what I hoped was the right length of time. Really too long—I got another beep, a long one, telling me I'd been cut off.

"Yeah, well, okay," I told a dial tone. "I'll tell him you want to consult. We'll wait."

Arnie came back.

"Gimme your car keys."

"I want to wait for Deke."

"Okay, but I need to go to the hardware store, and I wanted to move the car first."

"No."

Our eyes locked.

"You didn't get him," Arnie said, "and you're afraid if he sees the Toyota gone, he'll think you're gone, too."

I didn't say anything.

"I won't move the car, but let me get your gun, unless it's in reach right now."

I still didn't say anything.

"Goddamn it, Freddie, if I wanted to kill you, I could smother you with a pillow, and you couldn't stop me."

He was right.

"The gun's in the dresser, middle drawer. The clip is beside it."

I had to turn away as he delved under my sweaters, coming up with the Beretta and clip. I heard the click as he slipped it into place.

He pressed the gun into my hand.

"I'll be back as soon as I can."

Tears were sheeting through my closed eyelids and down my cheeks. I tried not to shiver, because it would only hurt my back.

Arnie let himself out and shut a door he couldn't lock behind him.

The phone rang.

"What the hell is going on? Can you talk?" Deke asked.

"Yeah. Arnie just left to get a dead bolt and some window locks. He wants to move the Toyota so it looks as if nobody's home. And he gave me the Beretta, loaded, so I think everything's okay."

"Shit. No way I can sleep. I might as well come back, see if he knows what he's doing."

"Yeah, well, only if you want to. If he was gonna kill me, he would have."

"He don't wanta kill you—but he's close to the person who does. And mistakes happen. I'll be over."

I lay there and stared at my dirty curtains. I couldn't turn the television back on because I needed to be alert for sounds. And I was afraid to shut my eyes. I didn't want any surprises when I opened them.

About twenty minutes later someone entered the house. I held the Beretta under the covers, aimed loosely at the bedroom doorway.

"Don't shoot—it's me." Deke peered cautiously around the edge of the jamb. "Where's your new boyfriend?"

"He's not my boyfriend. And he hasn't come back yet."

"Fine. Didn't seem right, him having a key to your dead bolt, so I figured I'd have to put one in myself. I'll get right to it—as soon as I move the Toyota."

I listened as Deke picked up the keys from my desk, went outside, started the Toyota, and drove off.

"What did you do with it?" I called, when I heard him come back in.

"I parked it around the corner, in front of the police station. I don't want something to happen to it, and your stepdaddy get mad at you."

"Thanks. Good idea."

Al was probably frosted already, just because I had the car. I wasn't certain things between us could get much worse, but I'd still rather return the car unscratched.

I listened some more as Deke drilled a hole in my front door and installed the dead bolt and as he rigged one of my windows so it would only open enough for the cats and most of the rest so they wouldn't open at all. I felt helpless, just lying there listening, and I hated that.

When I heard Deke stop pounding, Arnie still hadn't

returned. But neither of us mentioned that as Deke came back to the bedroom.

"I'm putting the car keys and one of the keys to the dead bolt in your dresser drawer," he said. "I'm taking the other key with me. I'll pick up some food and a toothbrush and be back as soon as I can."

"Toothbrush?"

"Yeah. I figure I better stay awhile. I got a couple of sick days coming, and I'll just lose them if I don't take them. Might as well take one tonight."

"You don't have to do that. I'll be okay."

"Lying here awake? Waiting for something to happen? No way. Your back won't get no better if you don't get some sleep. And I'm just gonna do it tonight—my back'll hurt as bad as yours if I have to spend more than one night on your couch."

"Okay. See you."

I was getting tired of saying thanks. I was as grateful as I could be, and being grateful was getting on my nerves.

Deke brought some chicken and coleslaw for dinner, and after a couple more pain pills I was feeling well enough to eat. Butch and Sundance smelled the chicken and appeared from somewhere, dancing around on the bed.

"I didn't get no chicken for them," Deke said.

"They can have part of mine. They wouldn't understand if they didn't get any. It's sort of a ritual, when I bring home chicken."

I shredded a thigh into cat-size bits, which I carefully doled out, one to Butch, one to Sundance. Then I took a quick bite of a drumstick. Sundance edged forward, and Butch swatted him. Before Sundance could escalate the confrontation, I tossed each one another piece. After quick comparisons, they decided each morsel was the same size, and it was okay to eat the closest one. Two small grease spots were added to the collection on my bedspread.

"Too bad they don't like coleslaw, or french fries."

"We're working on it."

When all four of us were finished with the chicken, Deke dumped the remains in the garbage, and I flicked channels on the television, looking for something to watch. I couldn't find anything, and I had fallen into that state of restless fatigue that seems to go along with having to stay in bed, so I clicked off the set.

Deke came back to the bedroom.

"You want company?"

I shook my head.

"Does that old TV set in the living room work?"

"Yeah, sort of."

"Holler if you need me."

I slept a little, off and on during the night, but every time I heard a noise, like Deke going to the john, I woke up sweating. He fed me more pills a couple of times, and probably I slept more than I thought.

The sun rose on schedule, and nobody had tried to get me.

The next time I woke, somebody was knocking at the front door. I heard Deke moving to answer it, and then Sandra's voice calling "Hello!" I felt a second twinge, not the one in my back. I tried to tell myself it wasn't disappointment.

"Hello," I called in return.

I heard voices in the kitchen, something heavy being placed on the counter. I started working myself into a sitting position, convincing myself my back wasn't as bad. I didn't want anybody carrying me to the bathroom. And I needed to brush my teeth, too.

"How are we feeling today?"

Sandra appeared in the doorway. She was wearing a purple denim jumpsuit with a white belt and white jewelry, and seeing her look chic and casual at the same time made me feel worse. Incompetent in all respects.

"Like shit," I told her. "And I gotta go."

"You look terrible. Do you need help?"

"I know I look terrible. And I don't want help. Please, go do something else. The bathroom isn't that far. And keep Deke with you."

"Okay. Yell if you want to. I'll have bacon, eggs, toast, and coffee ready by the time you make it back to bed."

I couldn't decide whether to say thanks or fuck you, so I

didn't say anything until the doorway was empty. This time I was going to walk.

I did, with the help of the walls. And I didn't yell. And I managed to lean against the washbowl long enough to clean my teeth.

I was just rearranging the blanket when Sandra swept in with one of those trays that sits across your knees, an official breakfast-in-bed tray. Coffee, a plate of bacon, eggs, and toast, and a small bowl of strawberries.

"Start," she said.

Deke slid past her and sat on the end of the bed, plate in one hand and coffee in the other. He put his mug on the floor.

"I already ate my strawberries," he said.

I started on mine.

Sandra returned with her plate and her mug. Deke moved over to give her space at the foot of the bed.

"What's next?" she asked.

"There's nothing new," I said, around a mouthful of strawberries. I had to remember to buy some strawberries next time I went to the grocery store.

"Except that the thug didn't come back," Deke added.

"What?"

"Arnie was here yesterday, said he'd be right back," I told her.

"What do you think happened to him?"

"Nothing. Arnie can take care of himself."

"Something," Deke said. "He wouldn't have let you down without something."

I concentrated on my eggs.

"Anyway, it doesn't matter. I'm a lot better today—and Sunday is supposed to be a day of rest—and by tomorrow I figure I should be back in business."

"Don't push it," Deke said.

Sandra nodded.

"I think you should let us do more. I'll talk to Juanita in the morning. Is there something else I can follow up on for you?"

"No. The only part that isn't dealing with the Marina

family is finding Stacy, and since Battaglia has to think I'm
out of it for a while, I'm going to try to do that through Dean
Sawyer.''

"By phone."

Deke glared at me over his coffee cup.

"Okay, by phone. I'll keep walking and driving to a
minimum, I promise."

After we finished eating, I could hear Deke and Sandra in
the kitchen for a long time. Deke was the first one back.

"You owe this woman," he told me. "Your kitchen
hasn't been so clean since you moved in. I picked up the rest
of the bird feathers out of guilt."

"Great. I know I owe her. I owe you, too. And I don't
know what to do about it except say thank you."

"You're welcome," Sandra said from the doorway.
"And I have to leave now. I'll call you tomorrow—don't
get out of bed until you feel like it."

Deke left shortly after Sandra, after dropping the Sunday
paper on my bed and assuring me he'd stop by later.

I read the comics and the headlines, but I couldn't get
interested.

I hate telephones, and I hate trying to do business on
them, but I finally decided Deke was right—I could at least
call Dean Sawyer, get Stacy's address by telephone.

Lily answered, told me to hang on.

"What's happened?" he asked.

"What have you heard?" I countered.

"Not much. Some kind of hassle between one of the
Marina boys and Battaglia, and somebody said you had an
accident."

"I did, and you haven't heard from me."

"Okay."

I liked the guy—he didn't push for an explanation.

"What's the skinny on the hassle?"

"Not sure. Some people think the Marina kid didn't
approve of the relationship between Battaglia and his sister,
some think it's about money, the one-third interest in the
corporation. My guess is it's the money. As far as anybody

knows, Lisa Marina loved her father, and any relationship with another man is probably business.''

''Maybe.'' That's a hell of a lot to love your father. ''But that isn't the reason I called. I still haven't had a chance to talk to Stacy—what's her name—the flight attendant on the *Odalisque*. I thought you might be able to give me her address, or a phone number.''

''Stacy Hallett. I've got a phone number. Just a second.''

He put down the receiver, picked it back up, and gave me a Reno number.

I thanked him, tried the number, and got a machine. I wasn't ready to leave a message.

Afternoon dissolved into evening. I flicked channels, tried Stacy's number, sat for a while in a hot bath, carefully tested muscles. They were better. This was going to be my last goddamn day in bed.

Deke stopped by with a couple of hamburgers, but I wouldn't let him stay the night. I'm used to being in the house alone, and having somebody around—even Deke— was making me even edgier than the prospect that somebody might try to get at me. Besides, he had fixed the house pretty well, so nobody could get in without at least making noise. And I would have felt more obligation than I could handle if he had taken off another night's work because of me.

It was sometime past midnight, when I had settled almost comfortably into watching Errol Flynn die with his boots on, that I heard a noise at the window. Butch jerked upright, and Sundance hopped off the end of the bed, preparing to slither underneath if necessary. I hit the mute button with one hand and closed the other around the Beretta, which was still under the covers.

''Freddie!''

The voice was hoarse, barely more than a whisper, but I knew who it was. I turned off the lights.

''Freddie, we gotta talk!''

''Fuck off,'' I muttered, just loud enough that I was certain he could hear.

''I couldn't come back when I said I would—I ran into

d'Azevedo, and I couldn't get away. This is as soon as I could get here without being suspicious about it. Are you okay?''

"I'm fine. I don't need you."

"Yeah, you do, but I understand. Listen, you gotta be careful—d'Azevedo's pissed, and he's taking it personally, that you survived the accident. Don't try to get to Lisa Marina right now, because he's got people around her. Don't try to do anything, except by phone. I'll tell him you're still hiding someplace—I'm supposed to be checking on you—but I don't know how much I can do, after tonight. Please think about staying somewhere else until this dies down."

"Fuck off," I said again.

Silence. For a long time. Neither one of us said anything. Finally, I heard something that I thought was Arnie moving away from the window.

Sundance jumped back up on the bed.

Butch settled down.

Errol Flynn had fallen off his horse with a couple dozen arrows in him, and somebody was selling used cars, so there didn't seem much point in turning the sound back up on the television set.

I didn't fall asleep until I was certain there was gray light through the crack in the blinds. Nobody would try anything a block from the police station when there was morning light, I was sure of that.

Still, I only slept a couple of hours, and I had a weirdly enhanced sense of what being alive meant when I woke up, gun in hand, and knew I had survived the night.

Chapter 10

NEVADA IS NOT one of those places that inspires poets. Nobody would confuse it with, for example, Xanadu. The past is pretty colorful, I guess, if you're into western lore; but the Battle of Pyramid Lake isn't exactly up there with the Little Bighorn, although the Indians won both. Major Ormsby, the cavalry commander at Pyramid Lake, is supposed to have pleaded in vain to be spared for the sake of his wife and small son. History is silent on her fate, but my guess is she did just fine without him.

Today, the territory attracts some pretty good artists—deserts are as variable as Monet haystacks—and has started to attract writers—but the list of native ones slows quickly when you get past Robert Laxalt and Walter van Tilburg Clark. Clark's daughter was the only woman I ever talked to who could make the idea of cleaning shit off your man's boots at the end of the day sound romantic. Not that she ever did it. I don't remember what her husband did, but he wasn't a rancher. I think he sold insurance, or something like that. Nevertheless, when she talked about Nevada, I had visions of women crossing the desert, cracking whips over the backs of yoked oxen from the driver's seat of the Conestogas, while their men rode shotgun beside them.

All most people remember of Nevada history is the Donner Party—those would-be Californians who ate their dying friends to stay alive when they were caught by winter

150

in the Sierras. A seldom-emphasized fact is that most of those cannibalistic survivors were women.

I'm not descended from any of those women—or not that I know of—but I have some kind of connection with them, a link that comes from living in what used to be their territory. When I drive out to the desert alone, I sometimes think I can talk with their ghosts. Or whatever it is of them that endures. They lived with pain, they went on, and they never let it keep them in bed. No way was I going to be stopped by a little thing like a bruised back.

So the first thing Monday morning I called a friend at the telephone company who checked a reverse directory and gave me an address for Stacy Hallett.

The second thing I did was call David Troy.

"I'm sorry I didn't return your call sooner," I told him. "I'm afraid I had to take the weekend off. Have you actually talked with Lisa?"

"I thought you might have been hurt more seriously than you wanted us to know. Are you all right?"

I assured him I was fine.

"Chris talked with Lisa, but evidently she didn't say much—she still thinks Connie killed Vince, and she's angry at her brothers."

"Is Ricky there? Could I talk with him?"

"Just a moment."

I waited, listening to the noises on the other end, as Troy called up the stairs, as Ricky Marina answered another phone, as Troy hung up.

"What's going on?" he asked.

"I may have trouble getting to your sister, and I hoped you would help me. Do you think you could get her away from the guest house?"

"I can try."

"Okay. Let's aim for noon, the Wagon Wheel coffee shop."

"See you then."

The hard part was getting dressed. Once I was standing and walking, it wasn't so bad.

The Toyota was right where Deke said he'd left it, in

front of the police station. I eased myself in and had to wait for a moment before I did anything else. My back hurt and I missed the Mustang. Shit.

Stacy Hallett's address turned out to be a small concrete-block apartment building on North Sierra, within walking distance of the university, the kind students live in. She opened the door when I knocked.

She was still young and blond and perky, but I liked her better in jeans and tie-dyed T-shirt than I had in that embarrassingly short gold skirt.

"I remember you," she said. "You're the woman who landed the plane. What happened to your face?"

I had been so concerned about my back that I had forgotten about my face, except when forced to confront it while brushing my teeth. The wraparound sunglasses couldn't quite conceal a bruise the colors of a rotting nectarine.

"I connected unexpectedly with a tree. May I come in?"

"Sure."

Stacy's small living room held a gray rattan couch with dark blue pillows and a matching chair. An unseen cat had raveled one leg of the couch and had started on an arm. The rest of the room was taken up by two old-fashioned board-and-block bookcases and a Wilson Phillips poster. I glanced at the books next to the chair. Almost covered by a fiddle-leaf philodendron, *The Epic of Gilgamesh* sat on top of *The Odyssey*.

"Professor Hellman's History of Western Civ," I said.

"Yeah, I just finished it." She sat on the couch and gestured toward the chair. "He's boring, but it was an interesting course. Better than most of the general requirements, even if it was all dead European males."

I didn't feel like getting into the politically correct discussion. I sat in the offered chair.

"What's your major?"

"Business—finance, actually. I know the hot times of the eighties are over, but I figure by the time I get out there, the stock market will be coming back."

"I knew a stockbroker once—he hated it."

She shrugged.

"Retail would be a drag. I figure I'll finish my bachelor's here, go someplace like Wharton or Chicago for my MBA, and then go into institutional."

"Why wait?"

"Because UNR is cheap, and I have a job that isn't too much work and pays pretty well. That's why."

"Good enough. Good luck."

"Want some tea or anything?"

"No thanks. I just needed to ask you a few questions about the day the plane almost crashed."

"Why? You're not the FAA."

"No." I fished out a business card. "I've been hired to look into Vince Marina's murder."

"You don't think his wife did it?"

"No."

She looked at the card, then back at me.

"How can I help?"

"Did you see anybody connected with Vince or the Seraglio near the airplane or even at the airport that morning?"

She shook her head, then needed to toss her hair back over her shoulder.

"I was almost late. I got there right before you guys did. Dean was talking with that weird guy who handles the charter outfit. I hate the way that asshole looks at me, so I went straight to the plane."

"Did you notice anything unusual?"

She started to shake her head again, then stopped.

"I got out an extra coffee cup. I had one too many cups of coffee. It was because I thought the piano player was coming, too."

"Tommy Durant?"

"Whatever."

"Why did you think he was coming?"

"He was in the parking lot, getting out of one of those gold limos. I remember thinking it was funny, that he had driven it himself instead of having one of the chauffeurs drive him."

I thought about that.

"Getting out of, or getting into?"

"I thought he was getting out of it, but now I'm not sure." •

Either way, it didn't make sense. Suppose Tommy Durant was there. Why would he try to murder his old friend—and the rest of us—even if someone at the Seraglio wanted him to do it?

I was going to have to talk with Wynn Everett again. No way would he have missed a gold limo in the parking lot.

"Neither one of them saw you—Tommy Durant or Wynn Everett?"

"I don't know. I didn't think about whether they did or not. But the piano player wasn't looking at me, and I didn't go inside the building, so maybe nobody saw me arrive."

"Okay. Thanks." I started to get up, but then I didn't, and it wasn't just the twinge in my back when I moved. Something else had been eating at me, and she seemed as good a person to ask as any. "Listen, you said you were a finance major—can you think of any reason why a one-third interest in a privately held company would become terribly important?"

"Not really. But I could probably find out for you. I'm taking one class this summer, and I'll ask my professor. Ortwin, did you know him?"

"No. I didn't take any classes in business."

"Oh."

Her respect for me was suddenly diminished.

I eased myself out of the chair.

"Thanks for your help."

"No problem. And I'll call you after class tomorrow."

I looked around for the cat on my way out, but he still wasn't there.

Climbing into the Toyota reactivated the electric prod at the base of my spine, but I had to make the trip to the lake. If I hurried, I could talk with Wynn Everett and only be a few minutes late for the meeting with Lisa Marina. I swallowed two of Deke's pills and started the engine.

Tommy Durant. He had opportunity, both times. What

the hell was his motive? Battaglia had to have threatened him—I still believed Battaglia had to be behind it—and it had to be over something more than gambling debts. Damn.

As long as I sat up straight and didn't turn my head, I could drive just fine. Highway 395 South was a breeze, and the first part of 50 wasn't bad. But I was hurting pretty badly by the time I got to the Tahoe airport, and getting out of the Toyota was no fun.

Only a few cars in the parking lot, and none of them gold limos.

Tahoe Aviation was empty. I wandered over to the desk, and I was thinking about going through the drawers, just for the hell of it, to see if they held anything interesting, when Wynn Everett walked in.

"Miss O'Neal," he said, smiling with the good half of his face. "What can I do for you?"

"You can tell me what Tommy Durant was doing here the morning Sawyer's coffee was drugged—and why you haven't mentioned it to anyone."

The turn from the desk to the door sent a spasm through my back so sharp that I had to grab hold for support.

"Somebody tried to hurt you, I heard that, and now I can see it. You don't look quite as pretty as you did the other day. Maybe you'd like to sit down."

"I just want to know what the hell is going on!" Sitting would only have hurt. And snapping at Everett was not going to help. "Anyway, you're better off talking to me than the FAA."

"I'm better off not talking at all, Miss O'Neal. I still have half a face—and it looks like that's all you've got, too. I'm better off not talking, you're better off not asking."

The smile was a leer again.

"Why would Durant do it? Just give me a direction to go in, that's all you have to do. Nothing that will implicate you."

He thought about that, still leering.

"Slip into the Seraglio tonight and watch the show."

"Why?"

"That's all. That's all I'll say."

I thought about the show as I drove what was fortunately a short distance to the Wagon Wheel, a hotel-casino just a couple of blocks from the Seraglio, and of about the same vintage. I didn't want to be a sitting duck for Battaglia and d'Azevedo. Maybe something would come out of the meeting with Lisa, so that I wouldn't have to go.

Ricky Marina was waiting for me, in a red leather booth in the far corner. He was alone.

"She wouldn't come. I'm sorry."

"Me too. How am I going to get to her? Battaglia's goons are probably guarding the door."

"Yeah, well, I think she told me what you need to know, although I'm not sure how it'll help. She says she actually got there earlier in the afternoon without telling anyone, and she was sitting out on the porch, just catching the rays, and she overheard a conversation between Dad and Tommy Durant. He told Tommy not to worry, it was taken care of, that he'd changed the will. That was why Lisa waited until she could catch him alone, after the show—she wanted to find out what was going on."

"What'd Vince say?"

"That he hadn't changed his will at all. That maybe he ought to, but he hadn't. That was all he told her. And that it wasn't about Tommy, he said that, too."

"Then who was it about?"

"Ready to order?"

A waitress appeared at the table, young and perky, wielding her pencil with a flourish.

"I don't want anything, I'm sorry."

I didn't think I could keep anything down at the moment, that was the truth.

"I don't want anything, either," Ricky said.

"Then what are you doing here?"

I didn't blame her for being annoyed.

We looked at each other and shrugged.

"Come on," I said. I fished out a dollar and dropped it on the table. "Sorry."

Ricky apologized, too, and we walked out into the casino.

The bells and the buzzers made it harder to talk, but we found a quiet spot near the escalators.

"I don't know who it was about, neither does Lisa. And he hadn't changed his will—I called the attorney in L.A. this morning, just to make sure. Hadn't even talked about it. Lisa, Chris, and I pretty much split things, with some small personal bequests going to Benny and Tommy and a couple of other people. Just what we knew."

"Damn."

"What do you think?"

"I think I have the frame of the puzzle, but I don't have the top of the box, and I don't know what the picture looks like, so I'm having to match it one piece at a time, and it's rough because the sky and the lake are the same shade of blue."

He laughed.

"You have a message for Mom? I'm heading back there now."

"Yeah. Tell her to hang in. I know she didn't do it."

"Okay. Hey—take care of yourself. Your face doesn't look too good."

"And it doesn't feel too good, but it's better than my back." I just realized I'd asked a grieving son for sympathy again, so I quickly continued. "I'm all right, really. And I'll be careful. Thanks for talking to your sister."

I watched him ride down the escalator. He turned back and waved about halfway. Then I looked for a phone.

There was a message from Stacy on my machine. I called her back.

"I asked Ortwin, and he said there are a lot of reasons why a one-third interest might be important, but he thinks the most likely one is that the two-thirds owners want to raise more money without losing control."

"What do you mean?"

"Okay." She slowed down for me, ready to spell it out. "You wanted to know why a one-third interest might be important. You didn't say how many other shareholders there are, but let's suppose that one person owns the other two-thirds. Or a few people who always vote together, family or something.''

"Say one person.''

"Okay. So if the guy who owns sixty-six and two-thirds percent wants to raise money for some reason, he can only sell another sixteen percent or so without losing majority control, unless the other partner goes along, or is maybe willing to sell some stock himself.''

"Herself,'' I corrected.

"Whatever.''

"Why would he need to sell part of the corporation? Couldn't he just borrow?''

"Maybe. It's complicated—depends on what their debt-to-equity ratio is now. This is a bad year for junk bonds— not that it's much better for new stock issues. The guy is probably looking for some kind of private placement. And he might want the minority partner to be even more of a minority, you know? If he gets the other guy down to, say, a twenty-percent stake, then his control is a little more solid.''

"I think I understand. Thanks for your help.''

I closed my eyes and leaned against the phone. Craig Battaglia needed money. Whatever the plan was, Vince Marina wouldn't cooperate, and Battaglia thought maybe Lisa would.

I tried to get Sandra at the *Herald,* but her voicemail answered.

"Where the hell are you?'' I said, and hung up. Not that I was certain Juanita Holt would tell her anything.

And the most important question that had to be answered was how I was going to live until the nine o'clock show at the Seraglio. I couldn't drive home and back. I thought fleetingly of my mother's place, but even that was too far. Besides, I'd have to deal with Al.

I trudged to the Toyota, and discovered it had one advantage over the Mustang: The backseat folded forward, leaving me enough space to lie flat on my back for a while.

I woke up to twilight. And cold. Lake Tahoe cools immediately when the sun goes down. I had shoved a jacket behind the front seat. I pulled it out and put it on. The sudden movement brought tears to my eyes. My back was better—stiff, but better—and healing. Movement, however, was still going to take thought.

The good thing was that I was finally hungry. I went back to the Wagon Wheel coffee shop for a hamburger and coffee. I sat at the counter, but it didn't matter because the waitress Ricky and I had walked out on was long since gone.

I marked a Keno ticket, and a clone of the new girl at the Mother Lode picked it up cheerfully. I glared at her, not ready for cheerful, and her smile shrank a little. I lost that ticket and two more while I ate the burger and drank a second cup of coffee.

This time, there was a message from Sandra on my machine.

"Juanita wouldn't tell me much," she said, when I caught her at home, "but she really is upset about something. Benny asked her for help originally, and then Governor Reilly asked her to pull you off, I got that much, but that's it. Does that help at all?"

"Yeah, I think so. At least it fits. I don't suppose you have any idea what the connection between Craig Battaglia and Governor Reilly might be, or why Craig Battaglia might need money."

"I have no idea what the connection between Battaglia and Reilly is—except for the obvious, heavy campaign contributions. I could make a stab at why Battaglia needs money."

"Why?"

"Craig Battaglia has an operating agreement with the Grand Slam in Atlantic City, and the owners of the Grand Slam filed for bankruptcy two months ago. I don't know the details, or how long he carried them, but he could have a serious cash-flow problem."

"Yeah, okay, thanks."

One more time, I hung up and leaned against the phone. I still couldn't see what the picture looked like.

I nursed a beer and lost a couple more times at Keno

waiting for nine o'clock, when I hoped I could slip across to the Seraglio and catch the show.

A five-foot-eleven woman with a blondish lion's mane of hair wearing wraparound sunglasses at night doesn't slip across the street easily. I did my best.

The Seraglio casino may not be the intergalactic bar from *Star Wars,* but the crowd was diverse enough that nobody looked at me twice until I reached the door to the show-room. The maître d' nodded, remembering me from the last time.

"I just want to stand in the back for a few minutes, catch the opening," I told him, palming a twenty.

"No problem," he said, taking it.

I also wanted to stand where I could see if he let somebody know I was there—that was the other thing, he might have been warned to look for me. And in that case, the twenty wouldn't be enough.

About ten minutes later, the lights went down, and the maître d' kept seating people, and I didn't catch any signals being sent. The music started, the curtain went up, and the familiar whoops of the cowboys and Indians engaged in their smoky, pink-lit, semierotic dance of death filled the stage.

I couldn't figure out at first what I was looking for. I knew something was missing, but I didn't see what it was until the first Indian died. She was tall and beautiful, with long black braids and coffee-colored skin, she fell like a swan, and she was wearing a decidedly non-Indian bikini.

But she wasn't Demetria Jones.

Chapter

11

THE GUEST HOUSE was dark. I had parked the Toyota about a half mile away, just off the highway in the shadow of some tall pines. I walked as quietly as I could through the heavy bed of dried needles until I reached sand so that I could approach the house from the beach. I hoped I'd be less likely to set off dogs, walking along the beach. Only two houses intervened. Nobody barked.

I figured I could do what Lisa had done—sit unobserved on the deck chair until I was certain she was alone, then slip in. A dark night would have helped. As it was, a very fat, very silver moon had just cleared the mountains and seemed to be admiring its reflection from the water. The sand was as white and shiny and insubstantial as powdered snow.

I felt like a horse, trudging along, boots sinking almost to my ankles with every step. Still, no one was roused. And there was a certain comfort to the chair, once I reached it. I had been there before, on a sunny morning, and I felt less threatened on the dark porch than I had on the open beach.

I shut my eyes and waited for some sign of life. My bet was that with Masaka cooking in the executive dining room, Lisa had had dinner there with her buddy Craig and hadn't returned yet. Once she did, I would have to figure out how to get her attention without frightening her.

The living-room light roused me. Or I think it did. I had stretched occasionally to keep my back muscles from locking in place as the lake air grew chill. But I had kept my eyes shut most of the time, almost secure in the quiet night.

Two voices. The words were clear. I knew the man was Craig Battaglia. The woman had to be Lisa Marina.

"I don't want to talk about it anymore tonight. I'm tired. Please leave," she said.

That voice was also stressed, the words a little slurred, as if she might have drinking.

"Please," she added, softer, appealing.

"We don't have to talk anymore, honey. Just say yes, and we won't talk anymore."

Even hearing someone else called honey was enough to set my adrenaline flowing.

"I want to go home, I want to go back to L.A. and think about it."

"You shouldn't be alone now. You should be here, with me. God, Lisa, I've loved you for so long, and now, with everything that's happened, I just want to take care of you. Please, please let me."

I had my fingers crossed that she wouldn't buy it.

"I need time, and you're not giving me time."

She was starting to cry.

"Please, honey, please. I need you so much, I want you so much."

"No. Please, no."

But he had found the words. He sounded like Vince, and she was weakening.

"Yes, honey, yes."

The lights went out.

"Please, Craig, please don't do this."

But the voice was fainter.

"It's okay, honey, I want to marry you, I told you, I love you so much, it'll be all right, I promise."

That was all I could take. The sliding screen was latched, but I lifted it out of its groove. The glass door wasn't locked, and the light switch was beside it. He was on top of her on the floor when the light went on.

"Goddamn it, the woman said no."

Lisa's skirt was up around her hips, and her face was turned away. Battaglia hadn't had time to do anything with his own clothes yet. Except loosen his tie, and he had probably done that earlier, over dinner, to prove he was a regular guy.

"What the hell are you doing here?"

His face was mottled. He pushed himself up onto his fists, and Lisa pulled herself out from under him. She still hadn't looked at me.

"I figured the only way I could convince Lisa that her mother didn't kill her father was to show up and talk to her. What the hell are *you* doing here?"

He stood up and backed away, his mouth hanging open as he tried to find words. Lisa huddled on the floor against the sofa.

"I own this place, and you're trespassing."

"Two thirds, Battaglia, you own two thirds of this place, which is why you're trying to marry the other third."

"Goddamn you, I love Lisa."

"Maybe. I just doubt it."

He was so angry I thought he might rush me, so I stayed loose and ready, hoping my back would hold up. Hefting the screen door had set the electric prods going again. In the periphery of my vision, Lisa was straightening her skirt—a black leather miniskirt that didn't cover much—and sitting up. She peered at me over her knees, like a child.

"You're the O'Neal woman," she said. "The investigator David hired to help Mom."

"That's right. Do you want me to leave?"

"No. I want Craig to leave."

"I'm not leaving." Battaglia was starting to regain his cool. "Lisa, she's going to tell you lies about me, lies your mother wants her to tell, and I have a right to defend myself against them."

"Okay." I moved sideways toward the chair next to the sofa, still not taking my eyes off him. "Let's all talk."

Battaglia sat gingerly on the far side of the sofa. I eased myself into the chair, and the prods clicked off. Lisa stayed on the floor.

"You first," he said.

"This is too soon. I don't have all the evidence. I was hoping Lisa could help."

"Go ahead. Ask her."

Large dark eyes like her father's barely cleared her knees. They even had the same slight haze. Either alcohol or tranquilizers had taken the edge off her awareness. Her nylons had been torn in the scuffle with Battaglia, and a ladder ran from her right knee to her ankle.

"I think Tommy Durant killed Vince," I told her, hoping she was alert enough to understand. "Not your mother. He was at the airport the morning Sawyer's coffee was drugged, and he was here to diddle with the vodka."

"Why would he do that? He was Daddy's friend."

"That's why I need to talk with you. You overheard something about a will—about changing the will. I think it's tied in to that. I think Tommy wanted the one-third interest in the Seraglio, and killed Vince believing he had it. He also believed Connie would be blamed for the murder."

"But Daddy said it wasn't about Tommy—and why would Tommy think he'd get all that?"

"I don't know yet. And since Tommy's dead"—I looked at Battaglia, who raised his eyebrows in innocence—"I can't ask him. It has something to do with Demetria Jones. And now she's missing."

"Demetria had a baby," Lisa said softly. "She said it was Daddy's. I didn't believe her."

"When did you talk to Demetria?"

The words were cold, snapped, enough to startle Lisa out of her lethargy. She turned to Battaglia.

"The day I got here, the day they pulled Tommy out of the water, when I went back into the hotel. She found me, she was screaming about losing her lover, losing her father, all she had left was her baby, Vince's baby, she said. She wanted me to help her, I said I couldn't help her, I didn't know what she was talking about. She said Daddy was supposed to take care of her, take care of the baby, and it hadn't happened, and she didn't know what to do. I didn't know what to do. I ran away."

"Vince was her lover. You'll have to fill in here, Battaglia. Who was her father?" I asked.

"Tommy Durant was her father." He had turned to marble. "And yes, to your next question. She had a baby about a year ago, and she said it was Vince's. He didn't admit or deny, he just said to make sure she kept her job and her medical insurance. What else?"

"Nothing yet. Let me make a stab at putting it together. You need cash because of your problems with the Grand Slam in Atlantic City—which are probably worse than anyone is aware of yet. Vince wasn't interested in either selling his share or putting any more capital into the operation. You didn't want to risk losing control—from the little I know about Pete, *your* father, I'd guess your agreement with him doesn't allow you to let majority control of the corporation out of the family—which is why you need to marry the one third back. Connie Marina had tried to kill Vince, everybody knew that. That's the frame of the puzzle."

Battaglia wasn't even trying to look innocent any longer. He was bloodless, a statue that someone had draped oddly with clothes, and I knew I shouldn't say anything more, but I had started, and I had to finish.

"You approached Tommy Durant," I continued, hoping I looked bloodless, too, not frightened, though, I didn't want to look frightened, "who was an easy mark because of his debts—and maybe angry at his old buddy for fucking his daughter, fathering his illegitimate grandchild—and said to him, get rid of Vince, it'll be blamed on his ex, and you'll gamble free for life. You might even have added something about taking care of Demetria and the kid. Tommy tried—long-distance, of course, he couldn't face violence up close. When the first attempt failed, Tommy got a better idea. Get Vince to change his will first, leaving his share of the Seraglio to Demetria and the kid. Vince, charming alcoholic that he was, assured Tommy he had taken care of it when he hadn't. When Tommy discovered he killed his old friend for nothing but a couple of empty promises, he became a loose cannon, and you had to nail him to the deck. How am I doing?''

"You're no Scheherazade, Miss O'Neal. You can't tell a story to save your life.''

"Come on, Battaglia. You have no weapon, and I don't think you're going to strangle me. Besides, there's a witness, and you need her. This isn't your style.''

"But I do have a weapon." He turned toward the hallway. "Jack!''

D'Azevedo appeared in the doorway, gun in hand.

"Of course, this raises the stakes for Lisa," Battaglia continued. "She has to choose your story or mine, that's all.''

Lisa whimpered.

"And if she chooses mine?''

"Demetria and the baby are safe. If Lisa has an accident, I'll just have to produce a codicil to the will in Vince's handwriting, leaving his share of the Seraglio to his love child. Tommy's idea wasn't a bad one, and I think I could persuade Demetria to cooperate. Demetria is a very pretty young woman, but she knows her looks won't last forever, and her options are limited. Anything else?''

"Just one thing. What the hell did Governor Reilly have to do with this?''

The marble of his mouth stretched weirdly, just for a moment.

"What do you think? It's just a little quid pro quo.''

"You got me warned. What did he get?''

"Nothing. I'm a large campaign contributor, that's no secret, and sometimes it buys me a little more than access. In this case, a word to Juanita. Reilly didn't ask for details, he never does. Not that it did me any good. Or you, either.''

"No.''

Damn. I really had hoped for something more than the usual sleaze.

I must have looked disappointed, because Battaglia laughed sharply.

"What did you want—pictures of Reilly getting his

wienie sucked by a hooker? They exist, but I'm saving them for a special occasion. This was just everyday business.''

Battaglia straightened his tie, as if signaling the end of the conversation.

"Jack, do you think you can do it right this time?"

D'Azevedo didn't take his eyes off me.

"Let's go," he said.

Before I could move, a redwood tree in a white T-shirt loomed behind him.

"Aw, no, Jack, don't kill her," Arnie said.

This time d'Azevedo glanced back, startled.

I whipped the gun out of my boot and fired in d'Azevedo's direction. I didn't have time to aim, and it wouldn't have done any good anyway.

The bullet hit his right hand. He dropped the gun.

Arnie reached for it.

"Hey," he said, laughing, "you're a real Annie Oakley."

"Hold it." I pointed the gun toward his solar plexus, knowing I had to be lucky again if I had to shoot, even with that big a target. I could hit him, but I wasn't sure I could stop him. "Whose side are you on?"

"That's right," Battaglia said, pure marble again. "The stakes just got very high for you, too, Arnie. Whose side are you on?"

"I'm on the right side." Arnie had an amazingly wide, cheerful grin on his face as he moved away from d'Azevedo, gun in hand. "This time, I'm on the right side."

Chapter

12

"SO WHEN ARE you going to see him again?"

"Goddamn it, Sandra, I don't even know if I *am* going to see him again. The police are dropping the accessory charges because he's testifying against d'Azevedo and Battaglia, not just about Vince Marina and Tommy Durant, but about a couple of other skeletons on the shore as well, and he's hiding out so he won't end up too dead to come to court. Once he's testified, he won't stay in Nevada. So that'll be that."

"Did you think about hiding out with him?"

I thought about hanging up on her.

"No. While getting me might make Battaglia feel better, it wouldn't do him any good. And I think his attorney will manage to convince him that an angelic appearance is his best defense right now."

"I heard Roland Wence has been having such a good time at Lake Tahoe that he decided to stay and represent Battaglia."

"Yeah, which means that d'Azevedo will probably end up the only person in jail."

"What about the kidnapping charge—Demetria and the baby—how can Battaglia get out of that one?"

"Come on. That's a matter of simple economics. She needs money. Ricky Marina is trying to get his siblings to agree to a settlement so she won't lay a paternity suit against Vince's estate, but that'll take time, and Lisa's cooperation.

168

My guess is that Battaglia won't have a problem buying her off."

"That's too bad." Sandra paused, then added, "Are you sorry I got you involved?"

"Not at all. I needed the money. And David Troy came through."

My doorbell started ringing as I said good-bye. I got up to answer it, pleased that there were no more twinges from my back.

"Freddie!" Mom exclaimed, reaching up to hug my shoulders. She took a half step back—all she could manage in her tight jeans and high heels—and scrutinized my face. "Well, you've healed wonderfully, and if you'd just put on a tiny bit of makeup, you could cover the last of that bruise on your cheekbone."

"Yeah, or I could wear my hair over it, like Veronica Lake." I hugged back tentatively. "You look great."

She really did. Her bright red hair flowed over the shoulders of her silver-studded denim jacket, and if it weren't for the faint lines around her eyes and a little softness around the chin, she could have passed for thirty. Not for my sister—we seemed to have come out of different gene pools. Too much lipstick, though. Mom always wore too much lipstick.

Sundance trotted past me and started rubbing against Mom's leg, purring and meowing.

"How's my sweet cat?" she purred back, reaching down to scratch his back.

I looked over the top of her head at Al, who was standing near the edge of the porch, red-faced and uncomfortable, brown polo shirt pooching out over his belted slacks.

"Do you guys want to come in?"

"No, no," Mom said. "We just came to make sure you were fine and pick up the car. And we have to start right back—you know Al doesn't like to drive after dark."

Al did a little shuffle from the porch down to the step.

I handed Mom the keys.

"Thanks for letting me keep it so long," I said. "And thank you, too, Al."

She hugged me again, and he shuffled down to the sidewalk.

I promised to come see them as soon as I had a car.

Sundance dolefully watched them leave. He liked Mom. I'd think it was the hair color, but cats are supposed to be color-blind.

Walking to the Mother Lode, a little later, when the sky was a haze of neon against the night smog and Mom and Al were presumably safely home, I thought about cars. I was going to have to get a new one, and I was still mourning the Mustang. I didn't have the insurance check yet, but I did have David Troy's, and I could get something, if I could only decide what. Maybe the thing to do was just walk around the car dearlerships on South Virginia until I found something that looked good. With all the global automaker deals, it was going to be hard to make sure I was buying American.

Deke was at the counter, but we didn't have much to say to each other. Scaling the cliff and killing the little jackrabbit hadn't turned out to be much of a thrill, and I'd already told him what little there was to tell. I wasn't feeling particularly cheerful when I walked home after losing seven Keno tickets in a row.

I was cutting through the small park toward Mill Street when one of the trees came to life and fell into step beside me.

"Hi," Arnie said.

"You asshole. What are you doing here? You're supposed to be in hiding."

"Hiding was making me nuts. And I wanted to see you."

"Okay, you've seen me. Aren't they supposed to have a guard on you or something?"

"Hey, come on, Freddie, I am a guard. And who's going to see me in the park at night?"

"I am uncomfortably reminded of an old Jimmy Durante joke: 'Elephant? What elephant?' "

"I don't understand."

I could barely make out his face, but I thought he looked genuinely puzzled.

"It's okay—you had to see the movie."

We stood there awkwardly, unable to see each other clearly, not sure what to do.

"I'll walk you home," he said.

"No, damn it. Get out of here and get someplace where you're safe."

"On one condition."

I waited.

"Promise me when this is over, and I let you know where I am, you'll come see me, and we'll go out for dinner and a movie." He smiled, I could see that. "One where the female warrior carries a gun."

I thought about it."

"Hey," I said. "Maybe sometime we could even watch Joan Crawford and Mercedes McCambridge shoot it out over Sterling Hayden together."

"So it's a date?"

"Yeah, it's a date."

He melted into the nearest tree, his Cheshire cat smile the last part of him to disappear.

I don't know where he went that night, but wherever it was, he made it safely. They got him in broad daylight, as two short cops were escorting him into Washoe County Courthouse. Somebody with a high-powered rifle splattered his brains all over the steps.

So I was right. D'Azevedo was the only one who did time. A year for manslaughter, plea-bargained.

Craig Battaglia married Demetria Jones, and somehow, when everything was sorted out, the Marina kids decided that maybe the one-third interest in the Seraglio was a fair price to pay for no lawsuit, no scandal. A blood test proved the baby might have been Vince's, and they didn't want to dig him up to check the DNA.

David Troy convinced Connie Marina that Seville wasn't such a bad place after all.

Governor Reilly was reelected.

I bought a Jeep. I don't love it the way I loved the Mustang. My relationship with the Mustang was an affair, a gut-level physical attachment. This is like a second marriage, comfortable, we get along, a sensible choice, but there's no passion. No acceleration, either.

The other night I hit six numbers on a Keno ticket, paid a hundred bucks. Winning felt so strange that I didn't know what to do. I gave the money to the United Way, with a note saying it was for the memory of Arnie Lagatutta, who was a good man after all.